Tell Me Please, What's the Matter

Poetry & Prose

David Booth

Blue Cedar Press
Wichita, Kansas

Tell Me Please, What's the Matter

Tell Me Please, What's the Matter
poems and other writings by David Booth

Blue Cedar Press
PO Box 48715
Wichita, KS 67201

Visit the Blue Cedar Press website:
www.bluecedarpress.com
10 9 8 7 6 5 4 3 2 1

First Edition   May 2025
ISBN: 978-1-958728-37-6 (paperback)
Library of Congress Control Number (LCCN): 2025908607

Editor: Michael Poage
Layout/Design: Gina Laiso, Integrita Productions
Cover Art: Vivienne Legg
Copy Editor: Linda Michel-Cassidy
Developmental Editor: Catherine Brady

Printed in the United States of America

For Ingrid

Tell Me Please, What's the Matter
Prose & Prose Poetry

Preface

Tell Me Please, What's the Matter includes prose poetry, verse, lyric essays, vignettes, and some concrete poems. Any one piece can blur autobiography and fiction until it becomes something different. Any one poem may take the form of a landscape or a musical instrument. Some of this writing becomes ekphrastic when I invest people's lives, real and imagined, with my own interests in art and artmaking.

Hybridity is a need to steady what I can't steady. Only I don't need to. Born of poetry and summoned by poets in moments of doubt, *negative capability* helps poets observe themselves in uncertainty.[1] I write to perform this—the mutability of living; the vicissitudes of work life, love lives, secular and spiritual life, family life, political life, life on social media, and so forth.

Though the indeterminacy to some of this writing is reminiscent of some familiar literary experiments from the past, I did not set out to conduct experiments.[2] The prose poem is not a formal experiment anymore, and children have been making concrete poems at school for generations.[3] Suffice to say that I am drawn to elasticity in genre and form as naturally as a boy choosing colors and textures for an art project. Combinations of shapes and kind help me put words to the ineffable.

When I think of these pieces as speech, I remember at times trying to be funny or smooth, and circling back to serious questions about our

---

[1] The poet John Keats (1795-1821) first discusses "negative capability" in a letter written to his brothers George and Thomas on December 22, 1817. He writes of those instances "when a man is capable of being in uncertainties, Mysteries, doubts, without any irritable reaching after fact & reason" as what one thinks of as the zone of creative expression.

[2] Despite my fascination with Avant Garde writing from the last century—from Gertrude Stein to LANGUAGE poetry of the 1970s and 80s—I cling to "story," while allowing for gaps in narrative logic within and between some sentences and paragraphs. The pioneering writing that inspired my hybrid sensibility characteristically moves away from confession, autobiography, and conventions in storytelling in ways I do not.

[3] The curricular activity of kids making concrete poems in the classroom began in the 1960s, as the "concrete poetry" movement took shape.

shared humanity: Why do warmakers force brutal certainties upon vast civilian life? Why the political cruelties transforming old rhetoric into as-if-new ideologies? Why the ambivalence some men feel toward their own masculinity? What's in a long marriage? How long are friendships supposed to last? How will we shelter in changing weather patterns with our senses collecting more subject matter than we can process? *Tell Me Please, What's the Matter* offers no answers but elevates mystery over doom and curiosity above easy indifference in my search for the right thing to say.

Broken Stirrup

At seven, Trudi will this time or next time refuse on principle to get out
of the water. She never likes to go. Already, she needs someone to take
her seriously. The struggle grows less muted. Trudi's mother is one of five
parents, men and women sitting poolside, who watch the children swim.
Talking about a drowning not in this pool but down along the shoreline,
they're tense to dive in if suddenly their child can't keep their head
above water. Only Trudi's mother's bathing suit strap has broken and
must hang on by diaper pins dug from another mother's tote bag. Now
Trudi's mom is listening to the other parents discuss a dead boy's body as
rumor would have it, while Trudi explains to the other kids the rules of
underwater tea parties treading water. "Before you run out of air, come
up for air and blow air out to sink back down again. Talk with your eyes
and hands only. Avoid too hard laughter. Sit cross-legged and don't mind
levitating. Pinkies up to pantomime fine china." Her hair billowing up
like forests of kelp, Trudi ignores her pacing mother refracted overhead.
But whose point of view is this anyway, who suddenly says stuff about
kelp while Trudi, as if she were in another state, chooses ignorance?
Something could go terribly wrong. She could cry out without a soul
to hear her. Years ago, when Trudi's mother was a nursing student,
green, childless, she was called from the break room into an emergency
situation. Soon, an obstetrician was instructing a birthing woman
to push while she, at twenty, leaned her shoulder into the flat of the
laboring mother's foot in place of a broken stirrup. She was all but a
bystander there. The blood took her breath as the good news of a fetal
monitor gave it back, as the mother's mouth strained upwards and the
mouth of the preceptor performed knowing smiles and the doctor's
mouth blurred as it coaxed. "Breathe," someone said. But bloody the
gloves of the attendants there, blood on metal, blood on the blades of
the episiotomy scissors snipping a perineum. The new mother gulped as
she heaved, or the body heaved as she was simultaneously elsewhere and
yelling and not stopping yelling. "Breathe." Then it was time. Time to
push up from the wavy blue bottom, swim to the side, climb the ladder
single file, sudden goosebumps, peeling noses, fall into thick towels,
flip-flop down cobblestone pathways, curse in waves rising off molten
asphalt. When Trudi burns the back of her legs on the beige seat of a

suffocating auto and says, "We should stay at least until it's dark out," her mother recalls not her own daughter's birth but the inner thighs of a stranger terminating at the head of a crowning child a long time ago on a cold, bright morning.

Euphemisms for Seasonal Affective Disorder

The artist Tetsuya Noda (b. 1940) makes prints of such commonplace objects as dishes drying on a drainer, a tomato plant, a pile of laundry, and an ashtray stuffed with cigarette butts.[4] Butts because he worries about his son being a chronic smoker. What father-artist wouldn't unless he's a smoker too and inured to the risks associated with tobacco use? Then he should have his vice without bringing his son into it. Anything else suggests a level of codependency that some see as touching and others as neglectful. Could the artist-father and his son meet in the backyard to breathe in and blow out smoke, look absently at each other's hands and mouths, breathe in, blow out smoke, glance skyward past birds on wires at the mood of the sky, breath in, blow out smoke, listen for incidental sounds of neighborhood, breathe in, blow out smoke, smother butts under rubber soles to sweep up later? Everyone knows it's the son alone who smokes and not the artist-father, whose dirty prints double as anti-smoking propaganda aimed at his child.

Tom's second cousin Susan wants to know what his habit of arriving early reveals about his personality. What's he supposed to say? That when he's waiting outside the museum and she's late, he experiences a dreamlike understanding that he's living in the wrong time and place while looking in every direction to see if she's coming? That the stakes are high even if to the naked eye he's not suffering? She'll be here soon, and it will be fine, and they will see the Noda exhibition and part ways at five. On his way home he will go grocery shopping for what his mother calls essentials.

What's a mimeograph machine anyway? Can a mimeograph smell good like a cigarette smells good or are all chemical odors off-putting to almost everyone these days? Unless his sense of smell is compromised,

---

[4] Born in 1940, Tetsuya Noda is a print-artist and educator. Not only is he seen by many as Japan's most important living artist but he is also one of the most financially successful artists of his kind in the world. Though this is not strictly speaking autobiographical writing, I did see his work once while feeling depressed about my living situation.

Noda must take it in while mimeographing his photographs to make his stencils. He must breathe it in while affixing stencils to silkscreens to transpose everyday images onto washi (fine Japanese paper). In one image the artist-father's wife slouches in a Bergère chair. In another she undoes her trousers. In still another she kneels beside her kneeling husband with one of their children peeking out from behind them. Elsewhere a child kicks up into a headstand while in an adjacent gallery a translucent daughter rises from dining chair like ghost closely watched by everyone. When Tom asks Susan if the Noda process is overwrought, a little gimmicky, she thinks for a minute before advising him, when he sees the artworks for himself, to get out of the way of his emotions.

Seeking proof for Tom's sake of the artist's "deeply-engrained aesthetic consciousness" surfacing in the prints of Noda, Susan warns him that a rose may act surreally large. "Take a step back," she warns, "and look all around you." It's no rose though but the lower half of a daikon becoming the lower half of a pale lady, and the top, torso-like half, bushy greens. To impress him, it seems, Susan is calling this "biomorphic" as a segue into a discussion of a print of a pair of walnuts hung on wood, their husks split without revealing the fruit inside. Or it's the yonic peach hung in a pose of vulnerability beside a scene from a race riot in America, beside the temple wherein the artist-father converts to Judaism, I believe, beside an apartment building blurred in passing, beside the long road ahead, when the questions arises, Whose may be this bellybutton? Tom blushes not because he feels inexperienced but because, given the ordinariness of stuff, he's not always sure what he's looking at. He calls the picture forming in his mind "Twenty-something on First Date" in which he is the lone subject.

A snapshot of Tom as a small child weeping makes him laugh because he has no recollection of what upset him. Overexposed, he looks like he has the sun at his back and is in a sense being born from it. He won't share this with Susan for fear she'll think he claims for himself a special solar status. Suffice it to say that if he were a Noda publicizing his own aesthetic consciousness, he'd start not with that old photo but with a panorama of an overcast day containing long gray clouds, waterways carved into peninsulas, canal barges drawn by horses, channel locks of bygone eras. Why channel locks now? What's the old technology? Why low-lying houses with flat roofs squatting in bunches up from tawny surfaces? Where are the people anyhow? These are family dwellings with no signs of sons and daughters and never any mention of those true individuals who, overexposed in childhood photos, carry within themselves such features of the mythical imagination as a firebird, the phoenix rising. But this is a horrible waste of time, isn't it? If only he could slip out without Susan thinking he's a weirdo, he might at last formulate in his exposed mind an apology to a world that finds his love of the old, love itself, boring.

On days like today
I have only
Mom's shopping list
to go by.

{ shampoo / potting soil / mouthwash / oatmeal } "sound living"

Primitive Drawing #1

Kepler   gives **the silver-**
smith Heather the task of **making the**
model planets a machine will set **in motion be-**
fore discerning kings and magistrates.[5]   **For the first**
time in her professional life, she's bored wit**h model gal-**
axies and somehow presents the royal court **with a flaw-**
ed model of the illimitable. Kepler must still convinc**e them.**   **Hea-**
ther must swear she's still with the program.   Once ho**me, her man**
says to her, Hello *Sunshine.* She says, I had a hard **day. He says:**
Do you want to talk about it?   She: I need to be al**one for the time**
being. He: Nothing gets better by bottling it up inside of **you. She: Let's**
be quiet and stop being such good listeners. He: **But I want**
to comfort you. She: I don't want comfort. **He: Every-**
one wants comfort. She: Stop right there, daddy-**o. I know**
what you're thinking, but you're wrong.   **I don't be-**
lieve everyone hates me or that **anyone dreads**
my voice when I giv**e a thoughtful**
command. I had **a bad day at work,**
that**'s everything.**

"#HarmoniousRelationsThusLaidBare"

---

[5] A guy once told me that people in close proximity to the actual Kepler (1571-1630) suffered his halitosis. There's no way he could know this. Who is the "he" in that sentence anyway?

March Sentences in Response to Apples

Plunging his head into a bowl of iced water in a spell of unseasonably mild weather is the defensive measure a man training himself against anger takes to trigger a diving response, a slowing down of heart, if only he reaches the bowl in time and hangs his head in time. *Spoiler alert*—at the end of this, the scene is an olden-days autopsy done with crude instruments to inaugurate an age of discovery. But retreat for now to a middle distance to a guy hearing sirens—those mythical seducers I read about in high school, tinnitus, sound and color of emergent vehicles, whatnot.

To whoever made the coffee, it's delicious. I feel guilty standing next to the pot greedily drinking the one thing I'm meant to save for others. Anyone who knows me knows I'm a one-cupper whose cup I never finish as I am too distracted to drink anything down to the bottom.

To those who don't recall the names of birds but that bodies of sound fall from the trees in half flight to hop amid the headstones of our dearly departed, there was a woman here the other day, if only I could have seen her. Someone said she looked like Janis Joplin (1943-1970) if she, Joplin, had survived into the twenty-first century. In his youth the poet Michael McClure (1932-2020) gave us the lines "the machines are too dull when we / are lion-poems that move and breathe" and later wrote the lyrics for Joplin's a cappella song "Mercedes Benz" about a sedan as a God-given luxury.

It isn't ice in this version but apples bobbing. Engraved with names of potential lovers: Rose, Braedon, Fran, William, the cultivar Roxbury Russet reaches back to our founding hours where boys with the sun on their backs plunge their heads into gray tubs of water to bite after apples shooting away from them. Tubs and hoses (not folkplay of some colonists' children) are the topic of a freewrite one June day, when shirtless boys with long hair hold nozzles upright for one another in the making of fountains to sip from. See them kneel again, and bowing again brace themselves with hands on rims, and rising again with apples in their mouths whip their heads back lashing their sisters with grassy water dripping drops down spines wrapped in mothers' beach towels.

If he did not include in his notion of an apple the familiar story of some men alive in our times claiming reverse discrimination after not getting the jobs they were vying for, he didn't know how to. He was this close to asking modest men and women where they got the confidence of their sexual appetites when yet another question arose to stupefy him: What if a constantly culminating block of prose read like a horoscope gave you sense impressions of someone you would soon see for the first time in ages? Years ago, an influential person in my own life told me never to write out my dreams for other people's consumption unless they'd made cameos in the dreams in question. I dreamed last night about a reader of mine walking away with the secret knowledge that I had lung cancer. My not having this disease renders it a thing for interpretation, as does the fact that the spoken thoughts of wanderers never seem to populate in my mind an ecstatic world but occasionally a golden one whose luster is less fine than muted and whose figures are more often than not silhouetted and slow-moving.

Who knows what a quintessential American tree looks like if not a Great Redwood growing in an out-of-the-way spot hollowed-out for the hanging of stolen meat? A line of sight between two trees carries me over the rooftops of an upward sloping city while at my feet cut flowers carefully strewn to be spirit-lifters wilt in time for me to sweep the walk and stoop. When on my day off I write, "I remember thinking about God as a child," my wife touches my wrist to say, "Check your syntax, darling." I remember thinking as a child about God. I remember as a child thinking about God. As a child I thought, and today I remember a boy feeling mocked for thinking aloud about God while the exuberance he felt for geraniums was no problem whatsoever and no one person was mocking or wounded.

Upon Leaving the Botanical Gardens
(Golden Gate Park, San Francisco)

> The epileptic seems to be in constant communion,
> dumb so far as memory is concerned, with a general and
> dark source of being. One might put it that an ordinary
> person's is animal life, an epileptic's plant life. The
> animal person (i.e. the normal) having no certain source
> of dismay in himself, turns to artificial and collective
> forms of it, insists upon 'facing up to things' which he
> has himself created, and accuses those who do not wish
> to probe, read, write, and talk about these things, of
> 'escapism.' The plant person (i.e. one who is afflicted
> with a mental, physical or nervous disease) has more of a
> tendency to be an 'escapist' or 'wishful thinker,' etc., and
> to search for: 'Whatsoever things are true, whatsoever
> things are just, whatsoever things are pure, whatsoever
> things are lovely, whatsoever things are of good report,
> and if there be any virtue and if there be any praise'
> to 'think on these things.' So that an epileptic, if he
> is not born religious, is likely to become so out of his
> unconscious and profound excursions into infinity.[6]
>
> —Margiad Evans

When Lilith finally opens her eyes
to those calling across the range,
she finds they've gone on without her.
Bruce, Robert, and Leo in one clique,
Helen, Janine, and Ana in the peaceable other.

---

[6] Along with Bessie Head (1937-1986) and May Sarton (1912-1995), Margiad Evans (1909-1958) is one of my favorite prose stylists. Each writes vividly about her inner life. Sarton shows us how starkly alone she can feel and how she must manage her anger. Evans writes in *A Ray of Darkness* about the epilepsy that potentially foreshortens her life by decades. Head writes naturally about tenderness though she must exile herself to Botswana to get away from the system of apartheid in her home country of South Africa.

          A bit dazed at first,
a woman coming out of hibernation,
Lilith asks, "What do our mystical experiences
          tell us?"
"What's the most mundane question you can
          think of?"
When she finally catches up with everyone,
Venus is sitting in the interstices of dark branches,
Robert is going on about the tattoo he'll get
once he's settled on an image,
Helen is explicating the news of the day—
          "Surveil me," she concludes, "I'm not hiding anything"—
and Leo must contemplate his mother's need for a knee replacement,
when a fake femur mimics the natural shape of the joint in question.
          Bruce mumbling Shakespeare.
          Mostly Lilith keeps an eye on Bruce
who just a year younger is her kid brother.
Of him she longs to ask, "What do our mystical
experiences reveal to us? What is the most mundane
question imaginable?" For Little Bee
Bruha, Bru-bru, Brewie is like Caesar
with his falling sickness, epileptic.
At the onset of a seizure, he experiences *déjà vu*—
I slept here twice for the first time
and *jamais vu*—my bed is not entirely of my own making—
intermittently and in rapid succession.
          Says Robert, "Maybe a jaguar on my forearm."
          Says Leo, "Swimming would've meant no impact plus
                    cardiovascular benefits."
          Says Helen, "Then someone must define privacy for me."
          Says Lilith, "Such an intermittence,
          I've been here before/I'm a stranger,
is like reading a poem."

Lilith crouching
furtive
bewildered possession
suspended nude until
recently perplexed
interrupted falling
down emergent.
Lilith didn't know
how but she'd been spotted.
Couldn't they tell
she was having a private
moment?

     Bruce presses his ankles together,
thrusts his hands skyward,
and letting his head fall back,
recalls not Caesar's command
"Set on and leave no ceremony out" [*Sennet.*][7]
but instead, the ancient genus magnolia,
a subfamily appearing before the bees,
its trumpeting flowers evolved
to foster pollination by beetles.

---

[7] The line "Set on, and leave no ceremony out" appears in Act 1, scene 2, of Shakespeare's *The Tragedy of Julius Caesar*. Here Caesar commands that proper rituals should not be left out, and here a horn is blown.

Jaunt

> My feelings I like to conceal from the eyes of my
> fellow men, of course without any fearful strain to do
> so—such strain I would consider a great error, and a
> mighty stupidity.[8]
>
> —Robert Walser

Thigh muscles bind and move the femur, bind and move, bind and move, thighs give life to long bones lengthening. Why does an angel reach for Jacob's thigh? Why touch it? How many people have been born from a thigh? We want to know but know no one who can tell us. Who among us has suffered a serious thigh wound? What is a serious thigh wound compared to a charley horse? What is the thigh's role in impulsive, regrettable behavior? We're told the word femur means to engender but can find no record of this in old saw lit.

What little boy doesn't make the mistake once in a lifetime of racing through the crowd of a picnic on his exclusive plane of existence to hug the loving leg of another boy's father? Looking down at the boy, a new father whose beard gives the impression of a cat burglar promises to shave it off if he doesn't want to scare the new son half to death before they've gotten to know each other. He's looking less conniving by the start of night, when he discovers a mole on his chin the size of a fossil snake for a doctor to burn off with liquid nitrogen. "I loved my beard more than the face it covered," he admits to the new son, "and removed it to find a spot of cancer." The new son says he must grow it back pronto if he doesn't want to look like a sudden child locked in no one's memory.

A man carrying a car battery in a crosswalk holds it in his hands like a sling for lugging. Sixty pounds we guess and it caves the shoulders and the chest and, straining the face, pulls the body forward while we wait in traffic for the light to change. The cold sore on his lip squeezed open like

---

[8] From Walser's story "The Walk"

an old cherry to engender conversations about boys and the men they're becoming, we watch his swagger pass and accelerate.

A woman who can't see far enough in front of her to know what's coming walks on the sidewalk with the aid of a walker toward a coyote eating the entrails of a trashcan as lackadaisically as distractible homo sapiens with cups of clam chowder. The coyote hasn't relied on birds' eggs in ages. Animals make slurping noises. Do animals make slurping noises? "We worry more about the spread of zoonotic diseases," we roll down our window to tell her, "and less about wanderers devoured." "Anything can happen," she shrugs. The sidewalk where a coyote eating remains intersects an old trail stretching down to the coast through a non-native forest featuring Eucalyptus globulus, Pinas radiata, Cupressus macrocarpa.

When poet Rae Armantrout (b. 1947) ends her poem "Native" with the lines, "Here eucalyptus / leaves dandle, // redundant but syncopated," it's Lovers' Lane we imagine in the woods where the coyote lives and the old army barracks in the north of San Francisco stand. A footpath carved out by Spanish soldiers and missionaries after the Costanoans and the Californios is a shortcut from the Main Post of the Presidio to the Mission on date night in those first moments in the life of a city. A path for young lovers to walk, countless people walk it. Some are pueblo settlers and mission fathers and some are men with pointy muskets, game birds hung from belts, mess-tins, toiletries. Walking together and always apart, as individuals they can neither smell their own noses nor kiss their own mouths. But they can admire each other's faces and lean into each other's bodies. Given their numbers, at least one of them wears his emotions on his sleeve and is well known for how exasperating this can be. If he is brave, intelligent, honorable, noble of action, his fatal flaw, a family trait passed down through the generations, is his inability to imagine these same fine qualities in those of his own and other species who naturally and tactically dissimulate. He can never hold let alone cradle the suffering of others.

Opossum

The opossum on our front stoop is neither dead nor playing dead but simultaneously immobilized and trembling from its core. I put my hands up at first, defensively, and backing away through this boxy house of ours to call Animal Control, have a moment of clarity: I love you, Babs, I say to no one home. How could I ever live without you? Returning a few minutes later, I find the animal gone without a trace. "Your presence must have been the shock of life it needed," you write to me, "to crawl away to its final resting place." I scan the yard and peer into leafy depths of rhododendron. I shine a light under the house. You write that no animal dying a slow death will let me see its remains. Not if it can help it. From start to finish, the nature of every animal is akin to our own personal integrity. Think about it. Who's ever seen the corpse of a bear while traipsing through the wild? You'd have to find one someone had shot, and even then, shooters take their quarry with them. "Meet me at Gardenias, Babs, for an asparagus risotto," I write, "and a glass of riesling." "I can do it all and look great doing it," you answer, "if there is good lighting." How easily I picture you in your dark studio, surrounded by your clay figurines, doglike mammals made to look like they're in motion. Wounded bears crawl away to dusky groves to be drawn up into their heaven by the thousands.

Mood for a Day

Looking down from a balcony onto a blazing bright spectacle of some kind, she wears a sequined dress, backless, while he looks past her from deep inside their condominium not to what he can't see her looking down upon but what must be a smoldering planet. God how he hates a smoldering planet. Hating with every fiber of his being, he soothes himself recalling Madonna, who is Mater, and Mater who is Mother of the Lilies and the lilies who go with Lily of the Heart, to whom he says, "I commit myself to you."

It is the Year of the Woman and scientists have discovered seven Earth-like planets orbiting a star some thirty-nine-thousand light years distant. My eighty-one-year-old mother asks, "Will humans bring sexism to a new planet or can we start without it?" She holds in her hands a drop spindle to make fine linen. An abridged version of an endless book called *Mind: An Essay on Human Feeling* sits beside her on a basket with its knees up and chin propped on loose fists of inquiry.[9] She has stopped reading at the sentence "It is natural for a person reared in the atmosphere of European common sense to assume that the use of ritual in connection with the ordinary, daily chores—gardening, hunting, fishing, handiwork—must have a practical aim, and to ask a native of forest or veldt how his work would be affected if the sacred forms were omitted." A hundred pages from the end, she won't pick it up again. Refusing any and all companion texts, she works out her interiorities on her own in anticipation of the busy day ahead. From a fiber mass does life after all continue.

Recession can be a father of conscience. How should we work now that we're failing? Like our own mother making it work? By some kind of rotation? To amass a deck? To make an intervention? Portfolio-sharing? In saying, "Labor is a way of knowing," the artist Ann Hamilton (b. 1956) asks what it means to live and work inter-generationally.[10]

---

[9] Susanne K. Langer (1895-1885) wrote *Mind: An Essay on Human Feeling*, first published in 1962.
[10] Like Noda and Neel in this book, Ann Hamilton is a popular artist. Known for her large-scale installations, public art, and collaborative performances, she explores the meanings of community.

What do you like about it? What's not to like unless you carry wounds from childhood and in your case such carrying is involuntary and unseemly?

The star at the center of the new solar system is called Trappist-1. True Trappists devote themselves to silence in the face of insatiable wonderment in the near and far of their wonders' objects. Its leash taut, a puppy called Prince Mutt gasps for joy and breath under the press of the collar against its throat as it strains to smell another's feces.

On a personal note, I'm happy to be going through life with you. It's a relief to sit beside you in a metaphorical cart that we may call Caring Cart Drawn by Mammals in our occasional practice of kenning upon a road grown less bumpy nearer the horizon. But what is an actual cart like? To my mind it is more practical than ornate when pulled by horses with minds of their own who treat us kindly while biding their time in their current occupations. In any event let us sit for a few minutes after some kind of communion and coughing stops, nose-blowing stops, throats stop clearing. The more palpable silence grows, the less cliché an ambience for self-reflection.

A Dun Forest

What's a dun forest in Blake's ode to an evening star, that "Fair-hair'd angel," Venus hanging in winter branches after sunset. What's dun itself. Why not look up dun and not let not knowing guide us. On a personal note, we miss a certain someone whose name we keep alive inside of us. We may never know if he's stayed away because he's dead or because, having taken up a second life in the wooded area north of here, he's as slow in growing tired of them as he was slow with us.

Watercolor, forest, grayscale. dun forest **NORTH** dun for dunforst dunfoerst dun furst done forced dunne forst dunne first dumb luck done fast well done dumb furst duhn ferst dunnforest dunstforst dunsfur dunsfern done for now forever done good enough dun forest dun fork dunforst dumb fuck dunfoerst dun furst dunne forst dunne first dumb force dumb furst duhn ferst dunnforest **EAST** dunstforst dunsfur done for now done dun forest dun for now dunforst first frost dunfoerst dun furst done last dunne forst damn fine dumb force brute force dumb furze soft touch duhn ferst dunnforest dunstforst dunsfur done well done now done late dun forest dun for dunforst dunfoerst dun furst dunne forst dunne first dumb force dumb furst duhn ferst dunnforest **WEST** dunstforst dunsfur done for now donewilling dun forest dun for dunforst dunfoerst **VENUS** dun furst done forced dunne forst dunne first dumb force well done dumb furst duhn ferst dunnforest dunstforst dunsfur dunsfern done for now forever done dun forest dun fork dunforst dumb fuck dunfoerst dun furst Dunsinane dunne forst dunne first dumb force dumb furst duhn ferst dunnforest dunstforst dunsfur done for now done dun forest dun for now dunforst first frost dunfoerst dun furst done last dunne forst damn fine dumb force brute force dumb furst soft touch duhn ferst dunnforest dunstforst dunsfur done well done now done late dun forest dun for dunforst dunfoerst dun furst dunne forst **SOUTH** dunne first dumb force dumb furst duhn ferst dunnforest dunstforst dunsfur done for now done willing

A trip into the wilderness was bound to last. We were bound to fail our inspections in falling light with failing colors though gray we say does not amount to failure. Our captors stand over us with soles of standard issue boots pressed squarely into our chests in the making of us into platforms. Our breath wheezes while somewhere close by a train clankety-clanks for metal knocks in passing. Smell of tar in the leaves, what blue between branches make, if we've heard enough of our own voices why not shut up already. Having faked swipes at our noses while sweeping our feet out from under us, at last foot is nothing more than a poetical unit of measure. We may never see you again but we can tell you this much: holes in canopies give us haloes tantamount to nicks and cuts of skirmishes as we go back one at a time to what we were doing. Peeking over the grass we see pup tents at base camp, tall trees circling a meadow, the sun not far from setting. Eyes we can't see stare out from trees. Those we think we see look like trees walking.

Ringtones

The birds we mistook for a ringtone, the larks in the birch beyond our window glass. Ringtones made the sounds of rain and the swish of the sleeves of strangers brushing. Water falls through the head of a tree, hard, deciduous. Tomorrow's forecast calls for ringtones rioting like spring flowers while we wait out the rain.

These boys like to hang out and talk to each other all day long, but it's never the two of them alone, as their phones are always abuzz and ringing. The one on the right, who uncharacteristically wishes to remain anonymous, texts god knows who after beating the one on the left, brainiac Tray, in a game of chess one Sunday afternoon. If there weren't something unknowable going on with him, he would gloat to Tray's face and Tray would ruminate on it behind forced smiles. What a novel ringtone this would make: the sound of a child gloating mixed with the softer sound of his friend, half-shy, gloating counteracted.

What I thought was a ringtone was the sound of my stepping whole-sole on the whole of my eyeglasses. If you haven't heard by now, it doesn't matter about the awful past.

What we mistook for a ringtone, the soft-scraping sounds of those brushing out their hair with plastic brushes. Rubbing scalps of enigma. What we thought was a ringtone was a source of causeless laughter. This is neither here nor there, but my niece's ringtone sounds like a flip-book animated snowdrift across a forest floor up to the earliest branches.

All day long travelers arrived from the front to be halted by an impassable river, so stand they on a muddy bank like figures out of a mythical literature. Frozen, drenched, far removed from cell reception, they watch the ferry and the ferryman going back and forth. They yell in vain their long-drawn summonses. One begs not the question, What is the Song of Deborah, but what is its melody, scoreless in Judges?[11] The

---

11 It's hard to know Deborah (d. 1067 BC). In the Book of Judges, she is a prophetess of Judaism. She is the fourth Judge of pre-monarchic Israel. The only female judge mentioned in the Hebrew Bible, she is a charismatic military leader who calls herself "a mother in Israel" (5:7). Though I see her as a courageous woman called on by the Lord to engineer the Israelites' defeat of the Canaanites under Sisera, full credit for victory goes to Yahweh (5:5). Her song suggests that ordinary people do extraordinary things. I don't know if Deborah is ordinary.

spiel I was going to give I believe I have forgotten. There's a forgetfulness in…. I forget where this comes from, but I've heard it said that a nuclear winter begins with a regional war fought with conventional weapons.

I read lips, you know. I'm reading yours now, while you explain to Little Boy Arnold the equations he must work out on the dry-erase boards around him. Up the hill from where I stand, a cordoned off area, ragged hill pine, falls into the ocean. The tearing sounds of collapse are not phones ringing. They say to the boy, "Show your work why don't you?" His reply: "I've done it in my head since the beginning."

The bodhisattva Guanyin is the one who hears the cries of the world.[12] She listens deeply without judging or reacting while he, who is he, talks prettily about shrubs. All the pretty talk in the world can't do justice to the long-necked birds and the boats bobbing between kelp beds. Ringtones ring out across this setting. What we thought were ringtones were kids these days using the phrase "Just saying" in their enjoyment of each other.

After two stressful weeks for both of us, we ran away for two days and a night to a yurt in the Salinas Valley. We forgot our phones. The springs of box springs called out coupling rhythms. Trouble seemed not to exist, or not to have followed us, like in these antique sentences from Steinbeck's *The Pastures of Heaven*: "The farmers at last lived prosperously and at peace. Their land was rich and easy to work. The fruits of their gardens were the finest produced in central California."[13]

What we thought was a ringtone was a wildfire. That the population of the world grew exponentially was one cause of such fires. What we thought were ringtones were human herds thinning.

---

[12] "Guanyin" is also "Kuan Yin" or "Quan Yin." In Sanskrit, her name is "Padmapani," which means "Born of the Lotus."

[13] John Steinbeck (1902-1968) is best known for his novel *The Grapes of Wrath* (1939) about the Great Depression. My favorite book of his from when I was a kid is his strike novel, *In Dubious Battle* (1936). Though the prose feels wooden now, at the time it made me feel like a successful reader.

He remembered he had a little pot on him, but it hardly seemed worth it. Every part of the landscape and sky, especially at night with stars multiplying and whining coyotes trotting somewhere in the distance, was like an outward expression of inner life.

It would happen several times that evening before he realized that the mysterious sound nudging him awake was the ice in the glass (on his nightstand) shifting as it melted. In the meantime, in the moonlight with the water slowly collecting, he closed his eyes, and getting this beautiful kind of curve, took up inventing again.

Primitive Drawing #2: "Do As I Do"

<pre>
Raise your right hand   and face the audience.
  Both your hand and your face open: stare blankly.
Turn your palm   out from the audience.
Your hand is an open face,   the term Janus-faced
  coming back to you from mythology.   Pass your hand
  across your face.   Smile,
      a new expression emergent.   You are happy for a time
        but pass it back again   to express sheer fright.
        Hold steady.   Pass again
          to show despair.   Pass: jealousy.
            Pass: compassion.   Work with anxiety,
            degrees of joy   veneration,
            lethargy   boredom,
            approbation.   I feel vulnerable right now,
          achingly so,   though I've wiped away
        the face of jealousy,   though I've been trying on
      dumb faces all day long.   How to finish as I started?
    A pebble I am collecting dust   in the bottom of a stream.
</pre>

The above drawing is meant to be the bust and hips and upper thighs even of a slightly crouched woman but has yet to surface. It is what it is. I count on my wife alone to discern my discus thrower at rest. In her downtime she folds forward with palms pressed together before her to imply as much or as little as a headless statue implies a physiognomy. My wife sees instead "a graceful pair of hands" and for this I am grateful. She calls my need to show her my pictures childlike. When I was truly a child and first getting to know my wife Helen, our fourth-grade art teacher Ms. Harvey sent us home with four-by-four-inch pieces of cloth, our personal yarn, our own needles, and baggies of cloth patches to sew onto our base squares as a way of making scenes of some kind. I was thinking of a super-closeup of a sunflower as being as close as one gets without troubling himself with realism when my father announced, "No son of mine is going to sew." I must sit this one out. In time I would grapple with a square of burlap measuring four feet by four feet plus foot-long strips to cut into any kind of being I could think of. Until then I would wonder where his initial decree sprang from. His forehead? His side? Is his elbow the locus of suspicion of what is feminine?

"Do As I Do"

Some Boys

Bylaws for a Boys' Clubhouse

One　　　What we celebrate here
We must do out there.

Two　　　We are hungry
But let none of us be exclusive.
We won't have just perfect people.
No one besides Kendrick Lamar is perfect
When he sings, "Don't give up, I won't give up."[14]
Though we don't know what other people believe
We don't ask of anyone, "Are you worthy?"

Three　　We are here because someone loves us
And whispers like Irenaeus
"The glory of God is a human being fully alive."[15]

Can we at least try to say this once a week?
To ourselves? To at least one visitor?

Four　　　In terms of how old we are
We are reaching childhood's pinnacle.
If we say to ourselves, "In ten years' time
We will only occasionally remember
What we've lived through,"
We may nod our heads in agreement
Without grasping what we're agreeing to.
These are our baby steps in shoes
Of seekers we're catechized to admire.

---

14 Lyrics from the song "The Greatest," by Australian singer Sia (b. 1975) from her album *This is Acting* (2016). The single features this verse from American rapper Kendrick Lamar (b. 1987).
15 From the fourth book of Irenaeus's *Against Heresies* (c. 200 AD)

<table>
<tr><td>Five</td><td>Every day is filled with pressure.
We must forget about it
Or breathing in and out and in again
Keeping it from showing on our faces.
If we're ever going to meet with the people
Who seem placed on Earth to guide us
And to receive our artless advice in kind
We must master not only our facial expressions
But also our rebellious natures.
We must learn to be more helpful.[16]</td></tr>
</table>

Two Boys on a Bed with a Guitar

Let's rock.
Say what?
I don't know.
You said it.
Said what?
Do you even know what it means?
My grandfather says it.
Why do you say it?
Everyone thinks I'm uptight.
What will you do?
I'll smash my instrument on a stage. [He rises.]
I'll buy a front-row ticket. [He drops to the floor.]
I'll throw my pick at you. [He throws.]

---

[16] Some boys hear some rap songs as the rude songs of hip hop, or it's singing and beats about social justice matters. With his antisemitic remarks, Kanye West (b. 1977) stirs up more trouble than most musical mavericks. Some boys think he's crazy. He'll say something like the soul music of the slaves is what the youth is missing about his own compositions. Some boys ask if they can forgive a singer of genius for his mental illness, turn their backs on him altogether, or find some middle ground in fandom. "Love'll get you killed," some boys sing like Lamar, "but pride'll be the death of you."

Will You Name Yourselves

> The dialectical notebook teaches the value of keeping
> things tentative. Without that sense, the allatonceness
> of composing is dangerous knowledge that can cause a
> severe case of writer's block. Unless students prove to
> themselves the usefulness of tentativeness, no amount
> of exhortation will persuade them to forego "closure,"
> in the current jargon. The willingness to generate
> chaos; patience in testing a formulation against the
> record; careful comparing to proto-statements and half-
> statements, completed statements and restatements:
> these are all expressions of what Keats famously called
> "negative capability," the capacity to remain in doubt.[17]

—Ann E. Berthoff

May my students now or may they never learn the power of negative capability to stomach lines like "The quadroon girl is sold at the auction-stand, the drunkard nods by the bar-room stove" from Walt Whitman's long gorgeous poem "Song of Myself." Who among them reads this without asking what's quadroon and why a drunk man nodding. Poet Allen Ginsberg describes negative capability, its name coined by Keats to explain what makes Shakespeare's humanistic writing as "the possibility of seeing contending parties, seeing the Communists and Capitalists scream at each other, or the Buddhists and non-Buddhists, or the Muslims and Christians, or the Jews and the Arabs, or the self and the not-self, or your mommy and daddy, or yourself and your wife, or your baby and yourself. You can see them all screaming at each other and you can see as a kind of comedic drama that you don't get tangled and lost in it, you don't enter into the daydream fantasy of being right and being one side or the other so completely that you go out and chop somebody's head off. Instead you just sort of watch yourself, and watch them in and out of the game at the same time, both in and out of the

---

[17] From Ann E. Berthoff's *The Making of Meaning* (1981)

game, watching and wondering at it…the ability to have contrary ideas in your head at the same time without freaking out.…"[18] Thus does my student Kurt call the drunk guy getting warm by the fire the alcoholic father saying the serenity prayer wet in his face the moment he wants to decapitate him: "O God and Heavenly Father, grant us the serenity to accept that which we cannot change, courage to change that which can be changed, wisdom to know the difference." Kurt is asking of quadroon and drunkard will you name yourselves or will the poet name you for us.[19] If too heavy an application of Keats' concept to our walkaround lives encourages a lowering of gazes, the literature tells us it makes for better writing.[20]

---

[18] From Ginsberg's essay "On Walt Whitman, Composed on the Tongue or Taking a Walk Through Leaves of Grass," collected in *Deliberate Prose* (Harper Collins 2000).
[19] "Kurt" is my homage to a young man who must be twenty-three now. In the spring of 2014, he was upset by the Islamic terrorist group Boko Haram's abduction of 276 mostly Christian students, girls aged from sixteen to eighteen, from the Government Girls Secondary School in the town of Chibok in Borno State, Nigeria. They had stayed away from school as a safety measure but returned that day to take their physics exams. "We ought to know their names," Kurt said, and he read from a list of as many as he'd gathered: Awa, Maryam, Rhoda, Rifkatu, Saraya, Margret, Esther, Malmuna, Amina, Glory, Hadiza, Joy, Moda, Tabitha, Baraya, Safiya, Rose, Rebecca, Laraba, Hanatu, Hauwa, Comfort, Yana, Godiya, Maryamu, Rejoice, Luggwa, Sicker, Zara, Lydia, Naomi, Rahap, Filo, Febi, Racheal, Grace, Abigail, Hajara, Monica, Docas…. Names of girls emerge ex nihilo to flutter here, momentarily incarnate, to alight where they will in whose memory?
[20] When I was getting my teaching credential to work in California public schools, I turned to Ann Berthoff to learn more about the pedagogical practices of Leo Tolstoy, Jane Addams, Paulo Freire, and Maria Montessori. Berthoff, who died in 2022 at the age of 99, wrote beautifully about teaching and learning. As strange as this may seem, this paragraph was inspired less by educators and poets and more by a flag some children made out of a piece of burlap.

Some Flags[21]

"Dear Friend, let me warn you somewhat about myself & yourself also. You must not construct such an unauthorized & imaginary ideal Figure, & call it W.W. and so devotedly invest your loving nature in it. The actual W. W. is a very plain personage, & entirely unworthy of such devotion." —Walt Whitman to Anne Gilchrist in 1872 in response to her offer to move from England to bear his child.

Being a man of his times doesn't mean he won't be scrutinized for his dealings after he is dead. Because he is a man of his times, upon passing may he or may he not be held accountable for whose perspectives he publicizes across his own and others' lifetimes overlapping. Men in their primes wonder how they will be remembered once they slip away to perpetual dreamtime.[22]

Accountable and unaccountable men close their eyes one last time. Those who close their eyes for a living leave us to wonder the moment muscles stop working who will do it for them. To counteract this darkness there is a travesty of ingemination.[23] I've only ever done it without knowing the word for it but love it for expressing what I am doing. The man ingeminates so much as to see it as a habit he must break or lessen if he is to relieve his students (I teach teens for a living) of the sound of his voice in the thick of an interminable lesson. My pet phrase I use with them as many as one thousand times daily is "Does this make sense to anyone?" I know it does because I see them working. Their running joke is to engrave it on my tombstone in the middle of the night when the guards are asleep and my wife, whom they will meet at graduation, hasn't beaten them to it.

---

[21] Vexillology is the study of flags, their history, symbolism, usage. Woodrow Wilson (1856-1924) speaks of flags as the embodiment not of sentiment but of history. Mine grow sentimental the more I write them. I leave out question marks in my wording of them if only because they look or seem like they should be declarative.

[22] The excerpt from Anne Gilchrist's letter to Whitman comes from *The Letters of Anne Gilchrist* and *Walt Whitman*.

[23] I wanted to sew the word ingemination into a flag indicating Whitman because I imagine him as a chatty fellow who is like a dry drunk outwardly sober but stuck in such old behaviorisms as always having to explain everything.

"I saw the three fish one head, carved on insole of naked Buddha Footprint stone at Bodh-Gaya under the Bo-tree. Large—6- or 10-foot size—feet or soles made of stone are a traditional form of votive marker. Mythologically the 32 signs—stigmata, like—of the Buddha include chakras (magic wheels symbolic of energy) on hands and feet. This is a sort of a fish chakra. So antique artists used to sculpt big feet as symbolic of the illumined man—before Greeks brought in human-face representation of Buddha. They never used to have statues of him— umbrellas, Bo-trees, or feet instead—before Alexander came to India." —Allen Ginsberg

Placed radially on the page like a pinwheel or some leaves conjoined in trinitarian configurations, three fish come at each other with mouths open as if pouncing on the same morsel presses their heads into a single encampment. I know what you're thinking. You suspect me of dwelling on poverty as an unsolvable mystery when in fact I'm remembering a boy from my youth. His father gave him the Rolex he'd lifted off his employer's body once the thing got appraised at a whopping twenty-four thousand and the boy had grown into a man who gives his wife the watch to hock for a tidy sum for her retirement fund though he must work to seventy. Ginsberg's utterances are all but devoid of fish in what I've culled from the body of his writing, he does send *The Catholic Worker* his drawing of three fish of a Buddhic nature along with a poetical caption to explain what we're looking at. The journalist and anarchist Dorothy Day (1897-1980) was uncovering the mystery of poverty when during the Great Depression she co-founded with a Mr. Maurin this newspaper and thirty years later who shows up but Ginsberg with his spiritual drawing. By then she was routinely reaching people through works of mercy like feeding the hungry, clothing the naked, visiting the prisoner, sheltering the ones with no harbor, and like that. She is poor because she gives everything she has as something distinct from negative capability and more like a positive capability to see both sides and a third side of the question of what am I doing. I will never see the fish as much as I suspect old messages of not rooting soon enough down in me. The brightness of the sun must be there when you're coming to the recognition of something painful and know with shadows of a doubt like shadows of fish flitting across seafloors that you haven't lived the way you were meant to.

[24] From *The Catholic Worker* (1967)

In Memory of Alice Neel (1900-1984)

When Lydia says that all police procedural dramas these days boil down to a policewoman determined to separate her estranged daughter from the older, violent criminal she's fallen in love with, she means Frank. He's the bad guy here. He's with her daughter Pearl now, and though he is older, it is in years only and not by way of any wisdom quotient.

She won't admit it but Frank suspects that for Lydia all speech is subtext more or less skillfully planted. If she's not presenting the plot of a primetime television show as a sublimation of her disapproval of his mannerisms, she's drawing on identity politics to uncenter him. This morning she spoke from across the kitchen island on varieties of invective in Dylan's "Positively 4th Street" and Swift's "Dear John" as if to question his ability to love a woman artist. When he complains to Pearl that her mother is at it again, she reinterprets the songs as Lydia's invitation into an intellectual conversation about them. Her main goal in life, after all, is to find one good thing about everyone.

Unconvinced he's welcome, Frank doesn't go with Pearl and her mother to the Alice Neel retrospective one Saturday afternoon in August. In their absence, he imagines Pearl alone with Lydia in a crowded entrance, where they don't speak but look at each other as they move with the others toward the turnstiles. Afterwards, Pearl will tell Frank about the obscure life of Georgie Arce, a boy from Spanish Harlem, whom Neel painted at least once in 1953.

If the meaning of the shape holds without Neel here to explain it, a Christlike pose shows Lydia and Pearl a tuberculosis patient dying for the sins of every passerby whose seeing can't be mistaken. Next, the 1936 painting "Nazis Murder Jews" depicts an anti-Fascist May Day parade in New York City. This is followed by Dachau survivors, German refugees, and a Jewish editor known to the artist and her writer friends. She does many portraits. Some subjects are curators and art historians. Some are new immigrants and others are migrants moving within the national borders and out from places, Pearl speculates, like the Jim Crow South. "Sad communities burgeon," she whispers in her mother's ear, "the more

in the open we visit." She's not sure what she means by this, so they
shelve it for the time being.

Lydia remains convinced that one of the more interesting cop shows
you'll find out there explores the ways a policewoman and her daughter
work out their love for each other using other relationships as their
proxies. This sounds wrong to Frank. "You haven't watched enough of
them," Lydia explains from across the kitchen island. From the next
room over, Pearl searches for the name of the boy seen in the Neel
painting. Because his story is one of crime, she's surprised some upstart
producer, cashing in on the art of reenactment, hasn't turned it into a hit
series.

In 1973, among faces of gay liberation, Neel paints the poet Adrienne
Rich with whom she argues what is proper feminism. She paints Jackie
Curtis who models for Andy Warhol, and Ritta Red, a drag queen.
Though the famous may fail in one's memory, Mother Bloor is here
too, and Kenneth Fearing is in an adjacent gallery. Neel paints aspects
of the avant-garde of her time with the conventionally salaried among
them. She does not leave out mothers, fathers, sisters, and brothers.
Though she is known for this kind of work, the word *portrait* makes her
squeamish the way words like moist and phlegm make others squirm.
But it isn't bodily for Neel: she calls portraits "pictures of people"
because the term *portraiture* belongs to an elite class in a way that a
billion selfies never can.

But Neel's favorite thing to paint is the nude. Who but the freest can
imagine sitting naked for Neel before she's talked them into it? We talk
ourselves and others into all sorts of things. Pearl asks, "Would you sit
nude for Alice Neel, Mother?" Lydia may not ask the same question
back because she's afraid of the answer. Thus, Neel uses the female form
to confront viewers with the physicality of motherhood, as many of her
nudes are pregnant.

One day the young Georgie Arce enters the artist's yard to say, "Ms.
Neel, can I play with your boxer?" Of course he can. Anytime he wants.
So he and the lady artist become friends, and this simple connection,
whether or not Pearl can articulate the oceanic feeling it gives her,

reaches into the twenty-first century. "They met when they had their whole lives ahead of them," says Pearl "and now they're gone, and I am alive, Frank." He doesn't resist saying, "Thanks for stating the obvious."

But Neel's most famous nude is the self-portrait she paints when she is an old woman close to death. With her spine erect and her eyeglasses pushed up to the bridge of her nose, she sits in a tub chair or loveseat holding a paintbrush as if poised to make a mark. She dabs with silver perhaps, if she dabs, as if to touch up her hair, gathered at arm's reach into a bun. She recreates her belly resting in her lap, her breasts resting, and the way she sits, her legs crossed to hide her genitalia. If her skin shows a blueness like flowering bluets beneath, her flesh is mostly pale and loose with some roseate shades and ruddiness to mark not only the worldview of a satisfied woman but also a flushness at the sight of her own body coming into view under her own hand. Alice Neel gives herself her discerning look in perpetuity.

Neel calls Georgie's intelligence penetrating while helping him to harbor the terrible secret that he is illiterate. With so many students and their needs, how can a teacher focus on a single child? It's Pearl who focuses now, standing back from him in the gallery. He wears maroon trousers, a light blue jacket, and a white shirt. His ankle boots bespeak dandiness, as do bright socks, and though it may not be a pompadour he's wearing, a tamer version of one adds to the precocity of his look. Pearl calls his gaze discerning like an artist's, but too grown up, and hates to see any young person acting seductive. But she may be wrong about this. It's a lot to take from a picture after only a few minutes, and she's never read body language very well and still less faces. But Neel does say somewhere that the boy, early on, absorbed an ethos that makes having money the one true thing for being alive in America. Soon he's mixing with gangsters in the city and living with them in Attica, and soon Frank is asking from across the kitchen island, "Was it robbery or something?"

Frank has a crime story of his own to tell, known to him as The Story of the Mole. Not the animal or a growth on your skin but a person posing as a cop to burrow with eyes unseen deep into a human precinct, now everyone must scrutinize everyone to see where the leaks are coming from. Once the mole is identified, one person after another steps forward to ask him why he takes so naturally to the secret infiltration of a community built on trust. To this moral question he replies but not until he's chosen his words carefully: "I am an outcast based on no evidence except how I feel about myself." Lydia and Pearl laugh their shared laugh together, so beautiful to see and hear that even Frank laughs.

Later, in bed, amid the regular flow of pillow talk, he tells Pearl she's beautiful and, predicting his insomnia will last through the night, he apologizes for carrying on so foolishly with Lydia. Because Pearl hadn't noticed him playing a fool, they collaborate in the defamiliarization of falling asleep as reaching a tipping point into blackness with light at times blowing around like curtains. Tossing and turning and getting up a few times to pace while Pearl sleeps, Frank vows to join her when he's ready. He takes a step back. They step back together to behold their own bodies, their legs splayed, their heads and sheets jutting in opposite directions, their chests rising and falling. To the sound of their breathing, almost imperceptible, the moon passes through a tall, slender window.

Greta in the Popular Imagination

Let's face it, you are not about to win anything.[25] Start with a current micro perspective. Those green governments standing by your side drown out the promise of minimum standards and a less symbolic politics of sympathy for ecological refugees. You may have won the hearts and minds of safe politicians but their everyday lives speak of you as a political cat video. (I apologize. That was a low blow, I know.) Concerning public debate, I can't help but hear your distress signal as small children calling from their beds for parents' goodnight kisses that despite your worst fears are forthcoming if you will let the grownups finish the mousse they're eating. Your way of shaming in broad daylight parents real and metaphorical leads to still more polarization when in fact no one took your childhood from you. Why stomp like a giant through a world in which you are welcome? Why spread a conspiracy theory that says I should not be vaccinated with a capitalist pharmaceutical industry behind it when such Research and Development will give me in my overlong adolescence the sense of a ripe old age if I let it? This is not a poem I'm writing to you. Such a thing is by its nature less direct and more semiotic and this by dint of its operation as an amulet or transistor of intellection and emotion. A poem's words *I love you* recede like a kingdom of plants, *I despise you*, a herd of sickly animals. You are not the person I think you are. You are who I imagine.

---

[25] A distant and disguising translation from the Danish of an open letter to Greta Thunberg (b. 2003) that my dear friend Finn, an academic in Copenhagen, posted on Facebook. He will give the silent treatment for the better part of the year if he recognizes it because he'll think I'm judging him knowing that's what he fears most from people he calls friend. I love him like a brother. My initial thought was to draw a picture of a middle-aged man and a young woman arguing over who is responsible for climate change. But it begins before either is born and in time for all boys and girls to be born into. Thunberg is a part of a lineage of environmental activists including Celeste Tinajero (b. 1995) from Reno, Nevada, and Xiye Bastida (b. 2002) from Atlacomulco, Mexico, who are younger than Finn, who is my age and no spring chicken.

Primitive Drawing #3

A
me
rican
century
daydreams
about standin
g on   a ledge
dreams it time &
again enters a fire
man to talk it d
own off its one bur
ning question did yo
u come here on your
own or did someone
send you did you co
me here on your ow
n or did someone s
end you did you co
me here on your ow
n or did someone s
end you did you co
me here on your ow
n or did someone s
end you did you co
me here alone or is
someone with you d
id you come here al
one or is someone w
ith you are you by y
ourself most of the
time now are you b
usy are you busy all
the time now do you l
ive and work in isolation?

When a man living in and out of
a box runs to catch a bus, at the
very sight of him the bus driver
not only accelerates but is seen
to smile. The man running with
his box in his hands yells over the
traffic, "May your house burn
down & all your children in it!"

A child heard a man
talking on his phone
about   fuck-you
money. She didn't
know what kind of
money this was or
what you spent it
on, only that this
man   spoke   more
and   more   angrily
into   his   phone
while walking his
dog in his pajamas
at noon.

"American Century"

Something Ordinary

When our top salesperson is euphoric and leaving us to guess how
long a manic episode lasts, she can't stop herself from describing to
our customers her Fallacy of Dispensation. On the road between San
Jose and Carpinteria, selling the same Matching Widget she's sold on
a commission basis since the founding of our company, she says to
someone like Marion Blanchard or Kevin Kim, "The aggregate amount
of suffering across the lifetimes of any one soul is the same for each
soul. Don't you see? You must see. We suffer as much as we cause to
suffer," she spews at Leslie Kuhn, Nicholas Lake, Martin Brandy. "We
harm in like measure." All grace goes out of her when she talks so
fast. So breathlessly. Red cheeks redden. Her mouth all but glistening
gushes exuberance while those eyes, an unsettling show of internal
compartmentalization, soften into a look of despondence and nearly
deaden. We want to put her in a hospital, but with such phenomenal
numbers? She does quadruple the business those of us vying for second
do. "Customers," she explains in a quiet moment, "crave an authentic
buying experience," and falls silent when we ask how one makes this
happen. We stand the silence while she tells us more calmly about her
old-fashioned sense of seasons. "Hot is hot. Cold is cold. Mild is the
popular favorite in a procession of landscapes, see them now parading
gorgeous, heather, dark red, golden?" Soon the long Visalia summers of
her youth spring to life, bringing her around to baseball and her love
of the Rawhide, the farm team of the Arizona Diamondbacks, which
played at Recreation Park, a block from her family's house on Goshen
Avenue. She knows by heart the stats of every guy who ever moved up,
and those of the sad young men who did not. The shortstop Knudsen
gets hit wide and outside by a brain aneurysm. Who could miss a game
after that, she tells her clients, and weeps for Knudsen in plain sight.
And weeps for her mother Annette and half-brother Charlie whom we've
all met and know to be of sound mind and body. "We will all be present
at the end of the world," she tells Cookie de la Croix and Zach Minor.
"All souls combined. No one's left out of this going-up, our rapture. We
are there now. I feel it. This feeling I have," she says, "is indescribable."
None of us look her in the eye when she gets like this but fantasize about
rising through the ranks to Regional Manager, when we will gently lay

her off. For now, she is our safety net and our bread and butter, and we are her Sentinels of the Accelerated Imagination. Mess with her, call her mad even once, and see how hard, how fast we come down on you.

One Another

One
One wants to write
a poem called Communion.
I do anyway, and so
beg the question
of what to commune with.
Do I begin where poets have been known
to begin? That is, in darkness?
And throwing off darkness—
for how quickly one grows
sick of one's Self, so much self-pity—
move outward
toward the one person I care about most
to say something like,
What would you like for dinner?
When you don't look up,
I ask what you're reading.
You reply, "The novella Communion."
"What's the gist of it?" I ask.
"A period piece," you call it,
"about the Red Scare,"
only it's no one thing
the closer we study it,
set as it is in cyberspace
summing up every scare we've weathered.
"I'm composing in my head," I confess,
"a poem with the selfsame title.
Can I give you the gist of it?"
"Comfort food," you guess.
"For dinner?" I ask.
"Something warm," you request.
"Something thick," I counter.
"Something filling," we say in unison,
for at last we are together.
We never go to sleep angry at each other.
We hold fast against our resentments.

Another
His favorite subject in school
a history of sibilance,
epochs like action figures mobilized,
like world wars, old Russia,
samurai with their bows,
swords and dressy horses,
the son would skip the middle ages
if not for the Mongol empire,
when Kublai Khan gets gout
  as a granddad
the same as said-son's grandmother,
a wistful woman now, feeding herself
overripe cherries for a curative.
Hear how Grandma and Khan
confront boredom head-on:
"If I do not succeed," they say together,
"I must punish myself
by waking up early in the morning
and facing what of life I can."
Less stubborn when tired,
they come alive before dawn—
and live for a little while much easier.

American Atavistic

On my way out of town one night I stopped to pick up a hitchhiker who has turned out to be a serial killer. I tell him in no uncertain terms that I am far more than a brand manager. I have my wife and kids to consider. I have a soul wherein winged things rise like heat through an aesthetic seeing God in the wind in the trees! If I drive my friends a little crazy with an exaggerated dark side am I not a true patriot? Is not my most successful brand for a new style of hot-dogging? Do I not read my passenger right as a man starved for attention? He tells me his name is clearly a pseudonym. I nod my head in agreement. He tells his victims what is going to happen to them. "Contrary to popular demand," he says, "my mother was the confrontational one and Father with his flat affect indescribable." It's kind of funny. Why not forgive them? When he says, "My teachers were sleeping logs who couldn't let sleeping logs lie," not only does no one doubt him for a second but the idea has been rolling around in their heads for centuries. What they have a harder time swallowing is their own dumb knife. Small talk falters, taunting relentless. They becomes we when suddenly we pound the wheel and throw our heads back in laughter as if to say in our own inimitable way what could be so funny? We press cold steel against our Adam's apples. We rip our eyes out before anyone applies any real pressure. We take ourselves apart limb by limb in the darkness and in the morning pull ourselves together again unaware all the day long of our own majesty. Who can say to whom such fantasies belong or from whence such emotions are far flung when one daydreams of meeting force with force and every third time coming out victorious?

I Am Against Driving Myself Crazy

Here Beside Me. Not to be confused with the travel writer who, best known for his writings on Cuba, spelled his middle name with one L, G. Phillip Crams died one day. For years afterwards I told friends he was an etymologist (words) when in fact it was entomology (bugs). I was thinking it was words when I confessed to my wife during one of our fights a fear growing inside of me that I would never amount to anything. Though she never acted on it, she had been in love with this man who died. She hides her grief now that he's gone, and I think of him less often. Hold on. Here she is now, beside me, asking me a question: "What's the rule of thumb for determining the ripeness of flatleaf parsley?"

Robert Lax on Patmos.[26] James Joyce used to talk about writing as if you were sending a telegram and each word cost so much in the beginning. What you start aiming for. I am against driving myself crazy so let them grow the way trees grow and don't dig for them unless you're willing to deal with the regret that comes with trying. Dreams emerge this way. Packed with meaning they surface perfectly free without your coaxing,

I run smackdab into Today,
someone I fear is lying.

Once you give that a poem flows with you, what you become regular about is sitting down every so often to write. May you encourage the poem to join the flow authenticating itself within you like private benedictions. May the flow grow naturally into what you want to say to everyone. How often does anyone tell you in all honesty never to stop doing what you're doing for the sake of others' edification? Forming the habit of working on a project all the time now, good moments arise by themselves as happy surprises, not to mention graces. We must put ourselves in good graces to receive them. All this doing to manifest yourself in writing.

---

[26] Here is my response to a video I saw on YouTube about poet Robert Lax (1915-2000) and his time in Patmos (1993-1999). Thomas Merton (1915-1968) called him his favorite poet, or one of them, and Ian Hamilton Finlay (1925-2006) loved his poems too.

To the writer. "If you write for God you will reach many men and bring them joy. If you write for men—you may make some money and you may give someone a little joy and you may make a noise in the world, for a little while. If you write only for yourself you can read what you yourself have written and after ten minutes you will be so disgusted you will wish that you were dead."[27] —Thomas Merton

[27] From Tomas Merton's *New Seeds of Contemplation*

A question arises concerning what you most long for. What about this makes you uncomfortable? "Who wants to be found out," you say, "as a man who longs for things he knows can't happen?" What's so shaky about the ground from which contentment arises? Can we not talk openly about it as part of the New Masculine? "Who wants to burn himself up over half measures?" Did he who first rode the winged horse describe the animal's moon-shaped hooves before or after it threw him? "The wings made the thing more holy than fast and as seeable in the sky as Przewalski's horse across the Steppes of Mongolia." Does your longing live behind such trivia? Leave you propped on your elbows, looking up from the dusty ground? Forced to, how would you kill it? "I won't kill it," you say, "but let it have its way with me."

"Pegasus"[28]

Primitive Drawing #4

---

[28] I've been in the company of five horses in my lifetime, Randall, Grand Smile, Love Lost, Alison, and Hero, none of whom belonged to me. Who could afford a horse on my salary? Aithon, Phlogios, Konabos, and Phobos are four firebreathing horses who, immortal, hardly keep in the memory, let alone form there, as they draw the chariot of the god Ares like a speck across the eyeball. My nephew calls mythology bullshit. The Bureau of Land Management in California, he once wrote for a laminated paper brochure no longer in print, manages wild horses and burros roaming over some seven million acres of public land. It seeks to maintain an ecological balance where maintaining includes thinning. Thinning is like the comic writer coming up with euphemisms for what he's doing. He says to his donkey one day that creative writing, like thinning, is the joy alleviating the pain about which he is writing. The range of the manuscript opens to contain everything at a slightly lesser rate than self-doubt begets erasure. No one on the planet is the arbiter of whether a concrete poem is working. I'm sorry I wrote it.

At the Height of the Pandemic (Days of 2020)[29]

A man called my wife a cunt today. She was jogging in the park when she pulled down her mask to take a breather. She wasn't the only one pulling down her mask, but she guesses she was oldest. Her gray hair, she guesses, made her an easy target. I said, "He fears the asymptomatic carrier." She said, "He can't bear the thought of a woman rule breaker." I said, "If I could, I would have a word with him." She said, "Why can't you listen to what happened without wanting to punch someone?" "I'm not punching anyone," I said. This was at the heart of the pandemic.

The Buddha sent his disciples into the forest to meditate for a lengthy period, months maybe, when complaining tree spirits set out to unnerve each neophyte. Why must invisible forces behave poorly? Buddha's response: the design of the ritual *metta* to spread loving kindness. You sit in silence as if for meditation, but instead of focusing on your breath or envisioning a tree in said-forest or a moon hanging in its branches, you speak within yourself, audibly to yourself, wishing for yourself good health and prosperity and safe passage through life. Say the same for your spouse and for those closest to you, mother, father, brother, sister. Say it next for your friends' sake and next to those you don't know as well but for whom you have an affinity. Spread it to people less familiar and those less familiar still, and on and on like this, that you may reach even the strangers of far distant rings, those most odious to you and even abstractions like Mussolini, who remain indifferent to the well-being of not only those close to you but also of the masses. As I write this I am reminded of Father Finley.[30] He speaks of grace as openness to the possibility that you could suddenly fall in love with everyone in the world. I used to think about this on crowded buses. I think about it now, in our time of pandemic, as empty buses pass.

---

[29] Rae Dalven (1904-1992), a Romaniote writer who grew up in the U.S., is famous for her translations of the poetry of Greek poet C.P. Cavafy. I read them when I was twenty-one. Many of Cavafy's poems have titles that begin "Days of…," as in his poem "Days of 1896," about the prudery of Alexandrian society wanting to quash his sex adventures. This strategy for titles, a rhetorical move, adds to a poem's timelessness, if only because a clear time marker interrupts any feeling of a poem being anachronistic.

[30] Dr. James Finley (b. 1943) teaches at the Center for Action and Contemplation in Albuquerque. He urges us to make contact with our divine in-dwellings as a way of overcoming feelings of shame, guilt, and doubt. May we know our true Selves at last.

Primitive Drawing #5: "Lute of Memory"

W
  ha
    t is
        t h e story
          of the lute
            of memory
          Is it more a
            n old string
              instrument
              or a shape-
                shifting object
                  —lute bowl g
                  ourd ladle spo
                  on shovel butte
                    rfly net banjo s
                  tretcher kettle mallet
                thought bubble frypan skillet
            objects for use by   all but not to be
          taken with us banner signpost sounding bo
        ard objects of the good kind of materialism s
      treet sign puddle light bur lap sack swatter quiver
        handheld periscope   blown glass pizza cut
      ter pinwheel fan fo   r fanning pharaohs b
      eaker vase thermo   meter stone outcrop
      ping across long p   ainted desert frond i
      t's tempting to bring   the plant kingdom into
      the mix more fully as a   way of opening the lute's
      secondary activity of   trans   mutation to also include ani
      mals so that in addition to   an igloo with a small   entrance
      and a long foyer one spots in spruce instrument tuber sweet
        onion spermatozoa rattle snake   digesting rodent these
          things exist in the realm of folk relative to anti mem-
            ory electronics and yet what can be more folk than
              the things folks use daily this lute of ours
                  is   at   last a digital camera

1.

"I play upon the lute of memory…. The strange thing is that when it sounds melancholy it makes me laugh, that when it is merry and leaping, I cannot keep from crying." —Robert Walser[31]

Or,

> "The idea of great distance
> Is permitted, even implicit in the slow dripping
> Of a lute. How to get out?
> This giant will never let us out unless we blind him.
>
> And that's how, one day, I got home."[32]

—John Ashbery

Or,

After Walser. That's how I make my living, through my music, he brags without bragging. I regret calling modest pride uplifting for now he thinks I'm enthralled with his being. I don't say this because of the slight irritation I feel when someone wants to talk modestly about their artistry in a way that we must sit around doing their boasting for them. I've never had a single bad thought about humble ambition. Nor will I talk modestly or boastfully about my having paid my way through life without help from anyone. This doesn't mean I'm like a true mystery on a higher plane than everybody. It means I will never see their modesty as false and mine as famous. All modesties are false relative to how realistic the desires of each individual show-person are becoming. You'll see what I mean once you stop using yourself as proof of the existence of the

---

[31] The Swiss writer Robert Walser (1878-1956) halted his literary career after being hospitalized at the Waldau asylum for schizophrenia in the final third of his life. The Swiss artist Adolph Wölfli was also institutionalized there but the seriousness of his condition was more discernible. Some suspect Walser of not wanting to live independently. This quote comes from his story "Lute" in *A Schoolboy's Diary* (tr. D. Searls).

[32] From the poem "Business Personals" in Ashbery's *Three Books*

selfless person. Who would believe you anyway if like music it's how to make a living? Unfortunately, when someone wants me to see them in a certain light and I'm letting my smaller Self color my thinking, I come across as conceited. But I don't care. Not really. If they want to speculate about what I eat, I must let them. Or they can ask, and I will tell them. Instead, they think to themselves without thinking that I am a vague noun and only later that I am a sentient being in time and space and thus proprioceptive.

2.

Coming of age, I drew the poet C.P. Cavafy (1863-1933) in my notebook in 1990 and beside him another poet, Frank O'Hara (1926-1966). Beneath Cavafy, for a caption I copied out "Of the Hebrews (A.D. 50)," which ends,

> His dedication was most ardent. "Always
> to remain of the Hebrews, of the holy Hebrews.—"
>
> But he did not stay such a man at all.
> The Hedonism and the Arts of Alexandria
> kept him their devoted child.[33]

To its right as you face the page, O'Hara's "Poem" begins,

> Johnny and Alvin are going home, are sleepy now
> Are fanning the air with breaths from the same bed.

Close to the end of the middle, the poet proclaims,

> There's too much lime in the world and not enough gin.[34]

---

[33] This is a poem from 1919 translated by Rae Dalven in 1948. See the bibliographic entry for "At the Height of the Pandemic (Days of 2020)."

[34] From an untitled poem that O'Hara wrote in the summer of 1955, the poem-entire, simply "Poem," appears in *The Collected Poems of Frank O'Hara*.

It has been over thirty years since I set eyes on these cartoon renditions of artful men. How old was I then, when I tried to imitate their poems, when in memory of my own budding sexuality, for I loved Tammy Toth of Milwaukee while wondering what a political awakening would feel like, I wrote THE DAILY RUB in big block letters on the opposing page and then an oblique scene, the origin and meaning of which I have forgotten:

> Setting aside urge and follow through, one experiences firsthand how polite the waitstaff is here at Café Midwesterner, and how polite those among us are in kind. The place fills with people saying please and thank you left and right while one takes in the picturesque beyond plate glass windows: wheat fields sloping up and up in the orange sky. Here too are the gauds of pop art: giant balls of recyclables call us to reflect on something big, like whole planets resting on their sides, when History and the old question of its trustworthiness appear in a daguerreotype fixed to a peeling wall: Lieutenant Colonel Platt's portrait and a placard to explain the boarding school he founded to the east, in Pennsylvania, called Carlisle Indian Industrial School (1879-1918). Bringing Oglala Sioux and Brule Sioux children forcibly from the Dakota Territory, and using the term *racism* in his advocacy for or against segregation, for his rhetoric confuses me like the term *right to work* muddles our ongoing conversation about labor unions, he was snuffing out more than kids' wardrobes and hairstyles.

3.

Finally does my drawing of young Shelley make him old because vitality is a hard thing to capture when you are drug-addicted.[35] He may be a

---

[35] It's Shelley I confuse with Coleridge whom my nephew misspells as "Colridge" in his emergent understanding of the difference between imagination and fancy.

woman the way I handled his features. If there's a better way, I'm all ears.
I mean really, unless one seeks a manual on how to make men better,
reading old literature one must replace in their reading mind the word
man when it could be a *woman* or all people with as complete an array
of pronouns as they remember to add a <u>blue rejoinder</u>. Watch me add
one now:

> The great secret of morals is love; or a going out of our
> own nature, and an identification of ourselves with the
> beautiful which exists in thought, action, or person,
> not our own. A <u>man</u>, to be greatly good, must imagine
> intensely and comprehensively; <u>he</u> must put <u>himself</u> in
> the place of another and of many others; the pains and
> pleasures <u>of his species</u> must become <u>his</u> own. (Percy
> Bysshe Shelley)[36]

                                 simply watching

for sadness overwhelms me

                  with

    the collective tolerates

             the decrepitude of

                    our sisters and brothers

---

[36] This is part of "A Defence of Poetry," written in 1821 and published posthumously
in 1840. Shelley was born in 1792 and died in 1822.

West, Evening (Regulus)

I hate art

Brendan draws a straight line but not straight but knocks the art cart down in frustration. What to practice first? Picking art carts up? Drawing lines straight? Calling it straight? Accepting failure? Injecting sounds and smells into a composition let alone a conversation? Critical look at cacophony? Evocative textures? Ode to color? When we were the boy's age and drew action figures with chewed pencils, we formed fists for them to push down deep into their pockets and raise out again, open in exuberance, while outside in the chill air, amid a spirit world reaching beyond the Milky Way, ordinary people oscillated between eternity and a perpetual state of longing-after on holy and let's just say not-so-holy afternoons.

Some Footing

At the edge of the forest, his sister complains that everyone—mother, father, all friends combined—hates her. How exasperating, the light she puts herself in. She receives more than her fair share of attention if not all there is of it. "The only way anyone will hate you," they step in with the trees now, "is if you make them." "How can I make them?" "By letting them know that you think they do when you know in your heart it isn't true. Now keep close. It gets a little steep here." "But even if I *could* make them," she finds footing now, "why would I?" He raises his finger to his lips but instead of shushing her complains that everyone, mother, father, all friends combined, hates him. How frustrating given how famous he is with the children and parents up and down the cul-de-sac. "The only way we're ever going to hate you," she says, "is if you make us." "Why would I?" She raises her finger to her lips to signal a kind of animal passing through their midst. If they stay still and quiet, she waves him in behind her, they might get a peek at it.

Solomon

I've heard it said by those prescribing communion with the divine that we who guard our mouth and tongue distance ourselves from calamity.

diktat

When I was a child, I was told two pet phrases, the one from my father to "speak now or ever hold thy peace" (Kerouac's way of saying it),

diktat

and the other from my mother that no one not now or ever likes surprises.

mother tongue

Is this what shrinks call a double bind when the fear of unsettling a stranger combines with a sudden quieting to habituate silence?

Ode to Failure

All juniors carry a sack of flour around for two weeks like it's a newborn baby boy. Their grades are based on the health of the boy as determined by the final condition of the sack at the end of the normal timescale long since established. Anyone choosing to spread around the contents of his sack as a repudiation of our timescale is put in charge of a new baby boy to be carried for a period of three weeks to a month depending on the attitude of the new father. Spilled flour results in a third sack, carried a month. If not then, it's over with. We're done with him. But that's not true, is it? We're never done with each other, so take notes everyone on the protection of a fragile being.

Timescale

A father explains to his son how the stock market works while they walk the trail around Percy Priest Lake. The whole time his father is talking, the boy can't take his eyes off an owl watching them from high in a tree. Such distractions irritate the father deeply enough that he climbs the tree to merge his own with the owl's being. The moon is in the tree near the end of daylight. As the owl lifts into the air, its wingspan astonishes the boy. The bird flies west to California.

Places everyone, please

A boy stands in a doorway watching his parents go back and forth over the cost of living. Will they notice his fashion? Pant legs pegged over pearly white tennis shoes. Canary yellow collar flipped up for extra pizazz. Though he's been at it all day long with a wet comb, his hair falls forward into bullhorns until he can smooth it back again with more water. "Ahem." He clears his throat two times with a space in between each time, like the negative space around an object. Father speaks without looking. "If you keep combing it, it will fall out like a cancer patient's." "It will not," says Mother. "How ridiculous." "And put your collar down," adds the father. "You look like a fruitcake."

The simple self

When it came to him, he passed. He forfeited his turn. When it came to him, he passed, only to grow more and more furious because no one else was forfeiting his turn and he had missed his chance.

Companion

See him there. She found him for a friend. They dress the same, they talk the same, and they both like to dance to the same kind of music. If she could shrink him, she'd put him on her shoulder. If she could shrink him, she'd shrink them both so they could both go every place together unnoticed.

Shadow Play

A mother and father in silhouette reach after a boy himself silhouetted in britches while a girl with a bow in her hair, shadow of girl once present, walks in the opposite direction unnoticed. Passing music and such incidental sounds as the mechanics of the good brother working rods and levers without stopping to ask if plywood should have a say in things. He's painted his proscenium arch light purple. How his voice is supposed to reframe the silence as a feat of speechless ventriloquism is hard to follow. It makes no sense to anyone when he explains that if we listen to shadows while he animates them we will hear their voices in the distance. A sad autobiography needs the movements of household objects. What is it though? What is it really? Calling it a coming-of-age story seems good enough for everybody. Calling it confessional is fine. Call it what you want, what you will, he seems to tell us. Would we mind if he started over again now that we understand what he's doing?

Somewhere Nice

When she asks him to take her somewhere nice, he reaches into his pockets to find half the money he thought he had, plus a piece of paper folded many times over and cut into the shape of a baby. Why not flap it open for festoons of babies? Negative space is after all the space around and between each little boy with his paper penis. Given such a crude decoration for a baby shower, one wonders, can seeing between slats of fences give true glimpses of mundane landscapes birds cross on their way to wherever?

Das Kapital

Karl's father realized early on that his boy was a wicked genius. He warned him not to waste his talents but to foster relationships with the right, like-minded people in the highest and not the farthest reaches of society. If he could please go upward and not away from—"Please Karl," the father exclaims—he and his Jenny might dodge a life of poverty.[37]

---

[37] Karl Marx (1818-1883) was a revolutionary socialist who gave the world Marxism.

We eat what we have

Parts of a long line of twentieth-century road-trip movies, *The Grapes of Wrath*, whose poor whites flee the Dust Bowl in jalopies, and *Easy Rider*'s hippies speeding by on choppers make an obvious double feature. When you live on the fringes you eat what you have. You go where you need to go. Locals overhear your freewheeling vernacular. They hear Hansberry's Youngers arriving at Clybourne Park when, armed with automobiles and axe handles, they go on the offensive.

Neither here nor there

Of three tomatoes dying on a vine, the lowest looks less like a tomato to his mind and more like withering gold or a paper flower. This reminds me: his hobby as a boy (he was my best friend for a while) was to dry hybrid tea roses of peach, pink, and yellow to make into magical bookmarks. Going through his stuff, I find one a lifetime later in his worn copy of Frances Yates's *The Art of Memory* (1966), a history of mnemonic systems used by orators from ancient Greece to the Enlightenment to memorize even daylong speeches.[38] This is neither here nor there. What I want to say is that our late fathers both gave interminable speeches for a living, mine to the Army Corp of Engineers and his to his fellow agriculturalists gathered once a year in a courtyard at a land grant

---

[38] Frances Yates (1899-1981) was an historian of the Renaissance and of esotericism.

university in Yolo County. "Broken teleprompter" was his dad's euphemism for not needing a script or any aids or enhancements whatsoever when speaking to a crowd about the tomato in Italy, the tomato in Central Europe, the tomato in Africa, the tomato in China, Spain's tomato, tomatoes of India, tomatoes in the eastern Mediterranean, tomatoes of the Americas. What bugged us about our fathers' speeches was their willful ignorance of what we called hidden beings. In my father's line of work this meant the bulldozer, backhoe, and crane operators. Hydraulics mechanics. Excavators. His father failed to mention families of farmworkers beyond intimations of suns rising over fields at dawn with everyone bent in the shadows. Never a call to table to listen to the utterances of Dolores Huerta: "We must use our lives to make the world a better place to live, not just to acquire things. That is what we are put on earth for."[39]

To come at me like that

Someone said to me, "Fuck you, Mister Didactic." I said back, "That's a lot of power to wield, to come at me like that. I wouldn't know what to do with it." "You're doing it again," said he who came at me like that. "What?" "Being Mister Didactic."

---

[39] I thought of Dolores Huerta (b. 1930) when I read Helena María Viramontes' novel *Under the Feet of Jesus* about Mexican-American migrants working in California's grape vineyards. I asked my wife, "Is the protagonist Estrella inspired by Huerta's life in the Central Valley?" She didn't know and, distracted by her own thing, suggested that I Google it. No luck. Viramontes was born in 1954.

Sarcasm of Joy

"I hate dolphins (Delphinus) for their nosiness and contamination of seas but mostly it's their flat affect and dullness of mind and spirit." This is our friend Alan speaking. His name and sarcasm of joy remind me of the actor Alan Alda (b. 1936) in the role of Hawkeye Pierce in the long-running comedy-drama M*A*S*H (1972-1983). It's about a Mobile Army Surgical Unit deployed in Korea during the Cold War, which ended with the fall of the Soviet Union but may still be going. I was a kid when it aired, putting me in mind of two essential facts: you can tell stories about the Korean War as commentary on the Vietnam War, where my own father fought. Also, triage means a ranking system by which sarcastic surgeons identify the most in-need and simultaneously savable from amongst an insane number of people bleeding.

Of a Beaming Photog

If someone told Jon he could have the best life imaginable but that as part of the deal it must already be over with, he would have to think about it. Here his wife jumps in to remind him that this goes against his stated goal of living more in the moment. He's not so sure about this. Would he not have been more present in his best life? Years later, while knotting his tie for him intimately, she looks into his eyes and says, "Russia bombed Kiev yesterday and a bunch of people died." He is here now, in his Sunday best, and feeling okay about life as for the living. Not only is our

beaming photog making him look like a
million bucks but he's reminding me of
something: how I admire a man who can
coax us into smiling.

Jack is Dead

Nice to see you again. It's always nice
seeing you. A couple things. Could you
send me Jack's phone number? He was
about to give me some free advice when
I lost him in a crowd somewhere. I can't
remember what the other thing was, but
it will come to me. Thank you, by the
way, for putting on the festival.

JFK Funeral Procession

The day after the assassination, our
teacher brought her own television set
to school and arranging its rabbit ears
until the picture came in clearly, showed
us soldiers transporting the President to
Arlington. They carried his corpse in a
horse-drawn wagon whose horses, snowy
white, were mythical looking. A flag was
draped over the coffin like we'd never get
to him while mourners lined the avenues
for miles after the dead president lay
in state in the rotunda. The First Lady
shrouded in black, her little boy wore
shorts in winter.

Constant Coda

Today is a challenging day but not so
challenging that I can't maintain a sense
of grace and a disposition of reasonable
expectation.

Catch

Two men stand in a passage with a ball
between them. One wants to play catch.
The other thinks the object is to throw
the ball hard at the places his opponent

can't cover, and in this way get the ball
past him. Imagine the frustration of the
man who means to play catch.

Public Elocution   Juxtaposing international news items
with the mundane

main event of my life—
the cadence

that is   Reality is
of my voice— the expression of personality

       like a poem
does not make like a work of art
for a very good story. —Rabindranath Tagore

Still, I persist.
I can't help myself

when speaking aloud overwhelms me
with the sensation of someone else

echoing these selfsame deprecations
in her own voice

singsong or monotonous
a thousand years hence

sonic reconstructions
of the times of our lives

her own and their ancient history
of the outmoded doctrine of nation-
         building

or for that matter
         nation.

Childhood Memory

Saddam Hussein was hanged yesterday.
Yesterday Mr. Hussein was hanged.
Or yesterday was the centennial
anniversary of his hanging
so many years to the day
said-dictator was taken down or out.

A headline at CNN.com announces
he was executed with fear in his face.
I for one would register a different
   emotion.
I joke of course darkly.
Imagine *me* a world leader of an oil-
   bearing century.

Crossing Brooklyn Ferry

What sacred book does a condemned
man, not the deposed leader of a foreign
country but his American counterpart,
hand off to a mysterious stranger at the
last moment? The King James Bible?
Gone With the Wind? *The Pet Goat*?
Piketty's *Capital in the Twenty-First
Century*? The vast poem wherein the poet
having once started out from Paumanok
proclaims in a long democratic line
deformed hereafter
      "Gorgeous clouds of the
      s   u   n   s   e   t   !
drench with your
splendor   me,
            or the men
            and women
            generations
            after

                              me"?[40]

Give of your voice freely

Across the street from a matinee letting out do they read together from a good book by Greenpeace Heads of Oceans about how to remove plastic from their diets. Hear it read aloud, hear it in the round, pass it around, hand it to any person giving of their voice freely, asking not who can live without plastic doodads in bathrooms, bedrooms, workplace, and transitions between places but who will turn at last to soda machines, bamboo toothbrushes, second-hand toys, beach-cleaning expeditions, and heartfelt storytelling. The book as an object is its own matter. It turns in their hands. If its plastic lacks the plastic of laminate, and it might, depending on who you ask, the glue of the binding remains in question.

Confucian Ode[41]

Discovering the identities of her birthparents wanes as a lifelong obsession for what there is to know. They're gone now. She and Ted have raised their own children. The silkworm-pupa pendant pinned to her lapel, the mingling zi, is

---

[40] Arriving at the gallows, Saddam Hussein (b. 1937-2006) entrusted a fellow with a mystery book, I wonder what. The fractured line comes from "Crossing Brooklyn Ferry," by Walt Whitman (1819-1892). Though it is about the optimism of Americans, I turn to it in my consideration of an endless war on terror. When word of the 9/11 attacks was whispered in his ear, President George W. Bush (b. 1946) was reading "The Pet Goat" from an exercise book to a roomful of second graders.

[41] This distant piece of writing is inspired by my adopted sister (b. 1972). The term "ming-ling tzu" (pinyin: "mingling zi") literally means "mulberry insect children" and concerns adoptees assimilating into family life without knowledge of their birthparents. I cannot, on my sister's behalf, confidently raise questions of race as the sole source of her lifelong search for a sense of belonging, but it plays a part. She told me when we were kids such things as "I am only white when I'm at home" and, mysteriously at first, "No one likes me because I am a Negro." This from my Taiwanese sister, whose nationality was clear to me from when I was five.

the mulberry insect child drawn from a
Confucian ode and surviving in popular
imagination into the time of her birth in
the Republic of China but hardly talked
about anymore:
On mulberry leaves the silkworm fed
when suddenly the silkworm's grub
the sphex trapped in her own nest.
Bring your borrowed girl to perfection,
O mother wasp!
To form her in your image
make her as good as best.
Convince her of the clade of your
prescription.
The wasp takes the young of the
mulberry insect and transforms her into
a baby wasp in the process of claiming
her as a daughter. You see, you seal the
mulberry insect in your own nest and
rapping and tapping on its papery combs
bray "resemble me, resemble me" until a
young wasp emerges. But changing the
ming-ling into a wasp is no supernatural
phenomenon. The matronly wasp stings
the mulberry insect and lays her eggs in
its stunned body, returning later to gather
the larvae that have always been wasps.

A.I. Authored

Starlight Mind keeps the innermost
sanctum of her heart shut to others not
because she's cold but because opening
it risks letting coldness capture that last
vestige of warmth within her. Inversely,
she keeps the innermost sanctum of her
heart open to others not because she is
warm but because opening it lets warmth
liberate all but the last vestige of the cold
inside her.

West, Evening (Regulus)

A bright star shines tonight beside a waxing crescent moon. A meteoroid begets a meteorite. With bathing suits waiting downstairs in a pile, must we go down and put them on again before climbing up again and leaping?

Wonder Woman Alights on Dominican School

Zhongshan District, Taipei City, Taiwan, 1972

Mom stayed home for me when I was boy. Home was Taiwan once
Dad made captain at the Taipei Air Station. Then Sister Mother, who
some called Sister Esther and some called Superior General, became
my teacher at Dominican School. If I was the only one to call her Sister
Mother, it wasn't a put-down but a natural association between abstract
nouns for family members. I learned much later that her real name was
Marian Caldwell (1915-2000) and referred to her simply as Marian in
my daydreams of the conversations we might have had if she'd known
me as a grownup.

I don't remember what Marian looked like except that the frame made
by her coif and veil made her face seem bunched-up in a way she'd
grown used to. I suspect I was also warping her appearance in the
countless drawings I did in my spiral-bound notebook of cartoon nuns
in different shapes and sizes. She's un-seeable now. I can't even find a
photograph of her in the yearbooks of our time. She's buried in the vast
cemetery along Chongde Street in the mountains on the outskirts of
Taipei. I remember riding my Schwinn Typhoon down the lanes there
long before she died. I remember drawing myself speeding along on
my bike, cherry red amid grayest tombs and the likenesses of nuns and
my gravestone rubbings taped into my nonextant notebook. I used to
ask myself if the ghost fear of Taiwanese boys was real. If so, were my
rubbings more like goading the very guys I wanted to be friends with?

I would give anything to see the drawing that made Marian my enemy.
I almost certainly began with a few light marks and, with an expanding
sense of purpose, patterned blue bikini bottoms with stars for a pelvic
region. After that, I must have given her go-go boots galore, a lasso of
truth, an eagle for a breastplate, bullet-deflecting bracelets, and a tiara
doubling as a boomerang when weapons needed knocking out of the
hands of perpetrators—say Cheetah's. Say Ares'. Say Genocide's. Behold:
The Circle.

Mother Sister found no Great Defender in a leggy triangle whose legs were different sizes but asked of boy illustrators dumb to how girls should be considered what their place was in Earth's meadows. Able-bodied and swift with her hands, she whacked my knuckles hard with a rattan cane for drawing a pornographic picture. Drawing blood on her third hit she caught hold of herself.

I don't think she would have hit me had I not named my patron. From her greater perspective, I was lying. After all, who would put anyone up to such an odious drawing? Mary Chang, who was littler than I, I called Nettles after a stinging nettle stung her on our way up the Junjian Yan Trail to Dog's Head Mountain one sunny morning. It was Nettles who paid forward a cup of ramen for the likeness of the superhero she must call Supergirl because she had trouble pronouncing *w*.

Marian, you would be surprised to know how often I think of you. I imagine you sometimes in the bustle of crowded squares, among commuters filling the avenues at dusk, your hunch drifting away toward its vanishing point. I sense your presence now in a picture at an exhibition at the Harvard Bookstore on Massachusetts Avenue. Known for such books as *The Gashlycrumb Tinies*, *The Epiplectic Bicycle*, and *The Beastly Baby*, writer and illustrator Edward Gorey (1925-2000) includes more than a few cutthroats and pied pipers in his drawings. His style is disarming at first, and then it alarms. We must look hard and, doubting ourselves, look again to see if he really is featuring a pedophile in what appears to be a cartoon for children. Our fear of what it may be, Marian, we sense in this untitled drawing—

Nettles
in heels
& cloche,
in pleated skirt
knee socks, & sleeveless blouse,
with sashes about her head &, about her waist,
a secular cincture flowing back like streamers—
leaps moon-high
to scatter tarot cards
in her wake,

and fly beyond the bejeweled fingertips of the fat man striding along a
kind of Edwardian Fifth Avenue in his fur coat and golden fedora. If
he longs languishing to tap that or snatch that or whatever such beings
do, my own imagination, Marian, has always been more puritanical
than sexualized. Never mind that the illustration is a canard of human
predation provoking us to reflect on the jurisdiction of fear and
reasoning. Never mind that Gorey probably got smacked for being
accidentally or naturally flagrant or flamboyant in his younger days.
Never mind how one pays for being who one is in a conservative epoch.
But I'm no cultural critic. I'm not even sure what I want to say to you,
so I'll keep it simple: I wish you were here with me at the exhibition. We
could go to dinner afterwards. The first thing I'd tell you, even before
we shared our opinions about the art, is that I've tried many times to
write a memoir about my childhood. In it, I report that you hit me three
times and that on the third time you drew blood. This is my flourish.
Though you did hit me three times, and though it hurt, I did not bleed.
I wanted the word *blood* to connote the fear I felt, and my confusion.
I've called the piece, my so- called memoir, "Wonder Woman Alights on
Dominican School." It is my "Supergirl" essay, too. I was talked out of
doing much with it because this superhero means so much to so many
women as to feel proprietary. Your heaven is like that, too. Proprietary.
I've never believed in it as a place to go, but if it is a place, I look forward
to meeting you there and walking with you over mythical hills into
valleys and meadows where fear is a funny remnant and boys, taken at
their word, are patiently redirected.

Cambridge, Massachusetts, 2004

Virgin Territory

Do elderly characters show up in the stories you write? If so, do you give them meaningful actions? When I was by myself and a virgin, I wrote with the sparse vocabulary of my imagination a story about a long-married couple in their late sixties having sex and spooning while reminding each other of their accomplishments together and apart. Pillow talk I'd someday call this. I've never shown it to anybody, for what could someone with no experience whatsoever have to say about intimacy? What a secret joy though to populate a fictional reality with what I hoped were common love patterns for me to one day grow into. About the time I wrote this my father was pushing me to read John Steinbeck, his favorite author of all time from when he was in his late teens, and why not? You could flip to any page of *Travels with Charley in Search of America* and read, "I stopped conversing with my dogs, and I believe that subtleties of feeling began to disappear until finally I was on a pleasure-pain basis."[42] Such words are ubiquitous throughout the author's catalogue, yet I have my misgivings. Politically and over time does he, like the author of *The Big Money*,[43] shift from left-leaning to right in terms of world affairs, to what the adult me calls fiscal conservatism? He comes out in favor of the Vietnam War as the shipping home of caskets forces everyone—hear me deploy my adolescent verse— to imagine fathers dying alone in foreign countries:

> all night youth made complaints against an order
> loving man
>
> if you're rather busy you needn't write me every time
> I know how it is up that way
> two days of snow up around home

---

[42] Once my father caught wind of my reading the Cannery Row novels of John Steinbeck (1902-1968), he mailed me a photocopy of the short story "The Snake," also by Steinbeck. I hated it. One of the guiding questions of my youth: "How can a great writer write such a bad story?"

[43] John Dos Passos (1896-1970) is the author of *U.S.A.* (1937), a trilogy that includes *The Big Money.*

year-round theater of migratory fliers
a limb worn smooth by men who sit there
an ash pile made by many fires

a remembered stretch on which I find myself a child
all quiet on a mountain bus except the singing child
my sisters in mind
reasons found for motion
Lorraine and I might get hitched
the return address is Fort McClellan

I took his hand and he took it away

my empty life weeps inside
the unfortunate need for word

he said instead that his was a good address

Before the Advent

It's the same drawing every time, a log hewn from his imagination and two misshapen boulders. He slaps it everywhere. That's what his mother calls it. He slaps it on any writable surface he can reach without exerting himself. The wall at home where she measures and marks his height once a year on his birthday, low ceilings not in stucco, the one lampshade not pleated, pillowcases, doors no one's watching, wings of paper airplanes, bus seat, rubber of shoes, his own itchy cast, pages of hymnals, his desk at school, walls around urinals, his binder if it's not part of his portfolio requirement, beige rocks in the landscape above the highway, places for strangers to discover long after he's drawn there. His mother takes pictures of these penises for the boy's father to analyze from his office in Chicago. "They are as consistent," he observes, "as letters in a typography font." Speaking as if she could never see without him, he takes a breath and describes boys around the world drawing as a hip hop reference the same exact penis. "But if you don't follow popular music," she complains, "how can you know this?" The only way of spreading she's familiar with is the phenomenon of going viral. Then she remembers her piano teacher from when she was a child telling her that girls were playing the same hand-clapping games on every continent on the planet long before the advent of social media. "Same rhythms, same hand sequences, same melodies, same toothy smiles, same joy of laughter," she enumerates for the boy's father, "but how does it get everywhere?" "Think of a phallus metaphorically," he offers. "It's about power." "He's twelve, Gil," she counters. But who can stop it now? He will express his fear of powerlessness to as many people as possible until a time when he has grown more spiritually androgynous.[44]

---

[44] The first draft of this poem was initially as much about (writing about) boulders as it was about adolescent representations of the sex organ. My inspiration: in his 1983 book of poems *Fracture*, Clayton Eshleman (1935-2021) writes, "…as a white Anglo-Saxon heterosexual male, I must confront the fact that what I represent as a social identity is the great boulder that must be rolled away from the entrance to the cave in which energies of the minorities of the world have been sealed." In the twenty-first century, the penis-drawing boy, grown to a man like Eshleman, arrives at coffeehouses to read aloud his poems about boulders.

New Barber

> All along the tendency to deplore the absence of more has
> not been authorized. It comes to mean that with burning
> there is that pleasant state of stupefaction. Then there is a
> way of earning a living. Who is a man.[45]
>
> —Gertrude Stein

What are a barber's tools plus some popular haircuts. Scissors are a given, and combs and brushes, and capes and covers, and crewcut, slick back, undercut, and swiveling chair with footrest, and mirrors for faces like stink eye and radiant smile, and one strop, and Caesar cut, and quiff and coloration and bowl cut, and butch cut and bangs and pompadour, and deep fade, and patchouli-, bergamot-, musk-, lavender-infused shave creams.

The wind parts a boy's hair in different places without his having run headlong into it. He parts it with a comb in still weather. He lies with a fresh cut in a tub of soapy water. When his erection starts up he presses it between his legs until only a triangle of hair shows. He lets it up and puts it away again. Lets it up. Puts it away. One puts it away in water lapping while his mother and father speak on the landing and wind whips his sister's hair around, blowing clouds in from across the ocean. Push clouds out of your eyes, a romance wants to say, and blink away the sun. She tucks tufts behind her ears and follows the ground to where it will lead her.

Though the amount of money a new barber holds relative to their expenses is concept *numero uno* in the realm of business-owning, let us not discount such foundational features as *comparative advantage*—when everyone does what they do best to make a living—and *opportunity costs*—an on-the-books valuation of the things you could have done foresworn—in the making of an enterprise and metaphors for sound living.

---

[45] From the section "Rooms" in her 1914 collection of prose poetry *Tender Buttons*

A boy so high he said "I want to show all that I am" made gorgeous incursions into and out of the first person losing meaning. This old trick works with any word or phrase you can say ad infinitum: apricot, tread lightly, tremolo, Capitol Dome, weeping willow, Martian man, beloved colleague, the enantiodromia of "I wish you were gone" and "Never leave me," today's melancholics' chuckles, lucky marriage, that hellhole Bakhmut everyone knows about, my never-heeded insistence, "It's the surface, Pat. Please let me finish." New barber wants to read *The Grass Harp* in this lazy-day fashion over the course of a long summer but who wants to travel back to 1930s Alabama with so much in our faces now that we can't process it.[46]

If you think you're going to change someone by the grace of your presence, well maybe. We must change over time in the presence of others but rarely from the force of their directives unless they have power over us and use if for dominion's sake. That we dominate ourselves can seem more likely. The new barber was convincing himself that he was the kind of narcissist who's too much on everyone's mind to live freely when a neighborhood boy in need of a trim and working out a new idiomatic expression came into the shop to say, "Are there any backseat drivers in your family." Speechless, the new barber takes a walk with a friend that night to hash out key differences:

> The moon is full and close to Earth tonight.
> It rises over Sandusky while sturgeon dive
> to Lake Erie's bottom.
> The moon lends lucence
> to clouds and sleeping men
> walking in the shadow of a Ferris wheel grandly turning.
> The giant moon shines on sleepy men
> walking barefoot in cool night sand
> eating burgers from paper wrappers
> while openmouthed sturgeon
> push snouts and barbels

---

[46] Truman Capote (1924-1984) gave us *The Grass Harp* in 1951.

through mud, silt, and plastic containers
in the sucking in of insect larvae.
Sleepy men walk with backs
turned to a turning wheel taken for granted.
Sleepy men sail like clouds
in their daydreams
in the spotlight of the moon
call each other Best Friend,
for they walk beside each other
betrothed
until they may find someone
with whom to procreate. Sleepy men
agree to attend
their twenty-fifth high school reunion
arm in arm
if they can get drunk first
and leave after one or two conversations
maximum.
Silence ensues. Silence includes
the muted voices of a distant carnival, clouds in passing,
sturgeon in gloom.
Sleepy men whose gazes tilt skyward
walk in sand
up to their ankles. Their conversation
as private as it is trivial,
soon the ground passing beneath them
is a coming and going of water
leaving tufts of whitewash
gleaming.

"But you are not mine, are you. I am not mine," he says. "What if I was
the great grandfather and you were the new barber seeking my approval."

Placket

Father walks out of his bedroom naked one day. He must not see me there if he's willing to walk around so free. I've only ever seen him shirtless by the pool in Clearwater, and now he stands in the kitchen wearing nothing at all. Watching from the seat of the pantry, I can't take my eyes off him. He must see me too or think I'm nearby. There's no reason for him to think I'm not home while he walks around the house we live in. Who can go naked without an observant son watching? As he turns I swear he's watching me too. Following him with my eyes I get to my feet and trail him from the kitchen to the living room because I do and don't want to see. He stands before the big window fronting the house like pictures hung in a gallery and drawing the curtains back, watches rainfall for what feels like an eternity. Our faces fading in and out in the glass, he opens the front door and steps out into the rain. The possibility of our neighbors watching us through their own windows doesn't stop him from transforming into a exhibitionist. He stands in the front yard for as long as his schedule allows, only it's his inner clock we abide and not a gold-watch heirloom. Time unending, and sometimes as tiring as pushing through muck, brings us round back to stare at our palm tree as if we've never seen one before. Clouds pass over. The rain lets up and starts again. I return to the house through the mudroom matching his gait. Once in his bedroom I watch him towel off and start dressing. He puts on the great gold watch first and then boxer shorts and socks. He pulls on his V-neck tee shirt and a pair of pressed slacks. He steps into shiny black shoes on this way to the mirror to comb his hair back. He doesn't say a word to me but tucks in his shirt, knots his cloth tie and, nuzzling the knot up snug with his collar, aligns the knot with the flap of his fly, his belt buckle, what we call a shirt's *placket*. Buttoning brass buttons, he inspects rows of ribbons before commencing with buffing of silver bars. He arranges his campaign ribbon and metal branch-of-insignia across a *lapel* he calls a jacket's prominent feature. Fitting his hat on his head and angling it just so, he climbs into his long coat one arm at a time and clapping his heels together says, Son, I'll be back at the regular hour. Keep an eye on things, will you? Sure Dad, I say, and following him outside, watch as he slips into a car driven away by stranger.

Our Neighbor Dorothy

The man who claims he got us together is no longer in our lives. He lived with Dorothy, whose preoccupation with death is unlike anything we've encountered. After Lou left for Montreal without her, we found ourselves watching her movements through the sycamores demarcating our properties. As a couple, we're an introvert. If it weren't for Dorothy's appearances, we would be a total shut-in. She's alone now and not so easy to get along with, but no one said it was going to be easy. We never said goodbye to this Lou character either. Dorothy's response: "Sometimes an angel of death comes to us to say 'Eeew' and floats back the way it came, mute, expressionless." She wants us to ask her to what extent it will resemble permanence, but we're not going to do it. Our fear is that one of us must go first. There's no good order. We've lost touch with Dorothy since then. We thought we would grow old together, the three of us, and why not? She lived straight back from our place on Ann Lane and took to us like an orphan when she found herself single again. Then she would call thorough the sycamores for simple things like a trowel, a trashy novel, a ride downtown if we're going that way. She told us over dinner one night that the opposite of death is flirtation, and we believed her. A few weeks later she moved to Fort Collins with a Steve and a Border Collie whose name is so typical as to escape us. With the drapes pulled off, one window broken, her old house sits empty in a tanking market. We're reminded that we don't need divine inspiration every time a difficult situation arises. How about a humble spirit and the grit of non-metaphysical effort? A lot of people have this. We talk about it often, even as our flirting days are numbered.

Blaming Nancy (The Edge of the Kitchen)

I'm not blaming Nancy. It's tempting but I won't do it. To blame her would be to poison the air between us and potentially to blow my cover. May no one's cover be blown tonight. May the air we breathe remain fresh and ample.

I'm not going to dance with Nancy. It's tempting, if for no other reason than to mirror someone comfortable letting go. I am learning to let go but to mirror Nancy dancing could lead someone to think I was mocking her. This is not the night to imitate a wild nature. I will never mock Nancy for her wildness. One may or may not fall in love with Nancy but one must never make fun of her when she puts forth one of her purest selves.

I will not play the blame game with Nancy but I will dance near her as her brother has instructed. Incorporating spin moves into my otherwise straightforward maneuvers allows my gaze to sweep the dance floor like a searchlight with no inclination to shine a light on any one dancer. Is this not nonchalance deconstructed? Does not everyone dance near everyone in intimate club settings? This club falls somewhere between intimate and overly spacious because it is less like a club in its architecture and more like a repurposed gymnasium.

I will not rest with Nancy after hours of vigorous dancing but I will rest nearby and close my eyes in gratitude for my own able-bodied-ness. I will not in the timespan of a breath reach the conclusion that a guy's sister is bent on self-destruction, but I will look at her, take the mental snapshot I've promised, an image realistic and unromantic enough that she might not mind my having it, and walk out into the night. On my way home, I will resist contemplating Nancy in any other way than one contemplates the unknowable life of a person just being. I will inform her brother that sis is all right. "I saw her with my own eyes," I will tell him, "and she could hardly be in a safer environment."

The Edge of the Kitchen. Sundays she goes to see a man, presumably a man, for two hours in the afternoon. When we first ask the identity of this mysterious figure, she says, "I must go." When we ask again, she says, "It will humiliate us if I tell you." Without asking who she means by "us," we accept as true the risk of a critical loss that, if we force it out of her, we will all experience. We let it drop. We take turns cooking. While one of us cooks, the rest of us sit on stools at the edge of the kitchen talking about whatever. Our lives are more boring than hers now. Before the day is done, we must settle-up with Comcast, figure out our rodent problem, skim rough drafts of students' persuasive essays (wherein they argue for or against an animal Bill of Rights), finish lesson plans for counterargument and rebuttal, and if the strength we now feel holds into the evening, write to her one last time to ask why we see less and less of her with each passing season. Is it really that we're so nosy? Or is it more generally because we don't know how to laugh and let our hair down? Along with our hair, have we lost our sense of humor? Grown as it were too heady? Let's face it: unless we instigate our every contact, we must either track her down on social media or grow used to her image as a memory. We miss her take on the world. We're going to miss her in a terrible way.

The
mountain
protagonist

In   **gets under my**

the last thing   **skin more than**   I

I read in *Mallet &*   **shrubs or cats can**   thought

Chisel, a snow-capped   **because its creator**   I'd been reading

mountain crouching in the   **withholds her what-**   the voice of a woman

circle of a low-flying moon changes   **ness until the final utterance.**   younger than I

its life by learning to trust in everyone's   am.

best intentions. Why this reminds me of
my late Aunt Mare and her fascination, both before a tumor arrived and after metastasis, with Adler's Infinite
Community, I don't know. But the good-sounding-ness of it all makes our author R. Stier's choice of a mountain
protagonist palatable even to me, a discerning reader of psychological realism.[47] Don't writers do as they please
anyway? Once they've thrown sentience onto everything and all things made persons, how anxiously a shrub may
await a verdict while some cat speechifies.

"The Mountain Protagonist"

---

[47]If Alfred Adler (1870-1937) was as big a deal in the field of psychology in the nineteenth century as Jung and Freud, he is all but unknown today. To cure his patients, he coached self-acceptance to a degree that calls into question the existence of what everyone understands as trauma. After attributing the term "Infinite Community" to him, I suspect that I made this up as the long-term effect of accepting ourselves in the company of others.

Reading Plato in Memory of Mary Oliver (1935-2019)

> Never will you find the boundaries of the soul by whatever paths
> you search, so all-embracing is the soul's being.
>
> —Heraclitus[48]

You love the nature poetry of Mary Oliver, and I prefer Hass'.
Something so simple as his "small brown wren in the tangle/of the
climbing rose…"[49] stirs my imagination more than anything Oliver
wrote. You call her poem "Wild Geese" a *permission poem*, when the poet
invites us not to be so hard on ourselves:

> You do not have to be good.
> You do not have to walk on your knees
> for a hundred miles through the desert repenting
> You only have to let the soft animal of your body
> love what it loves.[50]

Soon the poem is moving us into abstract realms:

> Meanwhile the sun and the clear pebbles of the rain
> are moving across the landscapes,
> over the prairies and the deep trees, the mountains and the rivers.
> Meanwhile the wild geese, high in the clean blue air,
> are heading home again.[51]

I want to ask, What do you see in spaces run together like this? What
does it feel like to go out into it? Whatever "it" is, I peer through
colorless weather, pretending to see as I'm supposed to see, without
really knowing. Because I can't feel this poem the way many others do,
let alone talk about it in terms of my own existence, I try to coexist with
those oral geese flapping high overhead in some slack V formation, in
enough light to swallow a moon with.

---

[48] From *Fragments*
[49] From "Cuttings" appears in *Human Wishes* (1989)
[50] "Wild Geese" was originally published in her book *Dream Work* (1986)
[51] Ibid.

Mary Oliver's hometown of Maple Heights, Ohio, covers five square miles of suburban Cleveland. A handsewn notebook she carried for jotting down her experiences in the woods of Cuyahoga County measures 3-by-5 inches and contains owls, an alder grove, graveyards, bright barns, mothers, fathers, blueberry fields, mortgages, cranberry bogs, a bear, robins, impressions of a Shawnee past, rainy seasons, egrets, lightning, a few kids running at dusk, first snow, mushrooms, lumbermen, quick Ohio creeks, a train whistle, passing neighbors, strangers passing, a buck moon, hunter's moon, wolf moon, sickle moon, strawberry moon, walnut trees, beech, sugar maple, cucumber trees, each thing waiting to be reassembled into proper poems.

Many of Mary Oliver's poems rely heavily on abstraction to transmit meaning. In "Wild Geese," we read: "Whoever you are, no matter how lonely, / the world offers itself to your imagination (...)." Nouns like *world* and *imagination* suggest universality like *peace* and *soul* in a popular lyric. In other poems from *Dream Work*—"The Journey," "The House," "Whispers," and "Landscape"—what I call *idea nouns* define experience while evoking in me little in the way of my living senses. An interviewer once asked Mary Oliver if she had a favorite word, and she said, "Love, Mirth, Praise, Constancy."[52] I don't know why but I have always bristled at the notion of universally applicable ideals. Even if "mirth" names something wonderful happening to someone at a particular time and place, its announcement as a concept may not reach into me the way the writer of "mirth" wants.

In many of her poems it feels like no one is there. Who is alone on a plain without a ground, without texture, without the sound of water collecting, odorous night falling? May I not call into question my own presence here? Give me instead a poem of and about bodies convivial, occupied, hollowed out, awestruck, shifty, damaged, whole, strategic, lovemaking, reverent, familial, orphaned, self-actualized, psychologically real, who regardless of outward appearances feel isolated. In his poem "Privilege of Being," Hass writes:

---

[52] In 2011, Maria Shriver interviewed Mary Oliver for Oprah Winfrey's website. Though I was convinced the poet was reclusive, she was willing to share things one would expect her to keep to herself.

one day, running at sunset, the woman says to the man,
I woke up feeling so sad this morning because I realized
that you could not, as much as I love you,
dear heart, cure my loneliness,
wherewith she touched his cheek to reassure him
that she did not mean to hurt him with this truth.[53]

Working out his own abstractions of love, loneliness, and truth, this poet moves in the opposite direction of Oliver in terms of how one reasons. She looks for her desired ideals in the world and names them. In more uncertainty, he assembles the words to imply those same ideals as complexes of emotion. A series of associative leaps leaving him to trust to discovery the outcome of close attention, his poem is something in flux, really. In "Privilege of Being," a man's discovery of the separate life of his spouse, her loneliness within their union, reveals to him his own solitude inside their love. In "Privilege of Being," after the man learns of his inaccessibility to his spouse's loneliness, we read,

And the man is not hurt exactly,
he understands that life has limits, that people
die young, fail at love,
fail at their ambitions.[54]

Though the poem opens with images of angels looking down from heaven and humans pressed together in gorgeous lovemaking, this is not like Oliver's insistence on the euphemistic glow of being, or the implication of an untroubled poet, but the setup for something quietly happening between two people. The ideals and shortcomings of love are not containable here. Love's gradations are too numerous.

The night I learned that Mary Oliver was dead, I had insomnia. I've struggled with sleep since I was a boy. While specialists suspect synapses misfiring in my central nervous system, I know without knowing of

---

[53] Robert Hass (b. 1941) is a Pulitzer-Prize winning poet who served as Poet Laureate of the United States from 1995 to 1997. His poem "Privilege of Being" appears in his 1989 collections *Human Wishes*.
[54] From Robert Hass' collection *Human Wishes* (1989)

some experience buried deep inside of me. What this means exactly I do not know, but if I took up Hass's deductive approach to language as discovery, I'd start with an abstraction like disappointment and say next that a boy survived a lonely childhood, and next that his parents could hardly comprehend such a hyperactive son seeming at times so introverted. I would leave out that the boy hated himself for the way he must embarrass them with his sudden crying fits and news of those ludicrous confrontations with those few peers he sought, always older. How old was he then? Years run together into a single self-profile. Soon the man is moving on from disappointment by way of the overlapping ideals of forgetting and amelioration. He is a grown man. After reading about the death of the poet, he goes in search of the copy of *Dream Work* a good friend gave him for his thirty-ninth birthday, only it isn't Mary Oliver he finds but (O beside P, P beside O) Archer-Hind's 1883 translation of *The Phaedo of Plato*. Stamped with its Dewey Decimal number, it's an old library copy with a brown cover mottled to look leather and, in what must be a Victorian era font, faux gold leaf for the lettering. The card tucked in the sleeve inside the front cover lists in each their own handwriting those who once borrowed the book from the Evanston Public Library, along with their checkout dates. How did their copy of *The Phaedo of Plato* get from Illinois to him, here in Dayton? Books move like cash moves and both seem nearly outmoded.

Once, when I was a boy, my Clover fountain pen exploded in my pocket, spreading a dark blue spot over the wren in the rosebush patterned on the upholstery of my parents' brand-new Beacon Hill sofa. How did my parents react? My mother confiscated my guilty pen and forbade me from sitting on the sofa ever again. My father gave me a stern lecture then whacked me with a red oak paddle carved with a Latin phrase meaning perseverance. In reality no one said a word. No one touched me. There was no paddle. When I am eleven, twelve, thirteen, fourteen, and by then smoking, and by then drinking, no one disciplined me for staining, fabricating, cramming, eliding, spying, weeping, stealing, blaming, blame-taking, exaggerating, masturbating, hiding, dreaming of bullying, dreaming of loving, distorting, overdoing, underdoing, pacing, misreading, gaslighting, boasting, apologizing, gossiping, underreporting, flaking, overeating, anything. Without a word, they turned the cushion over to hide the stain I must check regularly, like I was its secret caretaker and it, my little being. Six months later, pulling up the cushion like prying a stone from a mud embankment, I found its underside pristine again with its wrens and brambles. So let two wrens perch in a thorny bush of my memory. Bird pattern repeats across the surfaces of the sofa without interruption. If I were a Hass, I would turn this pattern into a poem without the use of a single abstraction. I'd call it "Ruined Wren" and pour my empty heart out in it.

Plato's *Phædo* looks like a play on the page, a script in which so few players seem like too many, and too many speechify. The place of the dialogue is Phlius. The persons are these men:

> Socrates.
> Socrates's acolytes—Apollodorus, Simmias, Cebes, Crito.
> Phædo, who is the narrator of the dialogue to Echecrates of
> Phlius.
> Attendant of the Prison.

Convicted for both corrupting youth and irreverence towards parents and gods (asebeia), he drinks his poison with gusto from what I picture as a clay mug after convincing those acolytes visiting him in his jail cell of the indestructibility the soul. An old man's argument for immortality, it begins with a theory of abstract nouns, templates upon which his followers may fit their own lives in progress:

> Whoever you are, no matter how lonely,
> The world offers itself to your imagination,
> Calls to you like the wild geese, harsh and exciting—
> Over and over announcing your place
> In the family of things.[55]

Of our family of things, each thing inside it bears the name of an abstraction, an ideal object hovering in a heaven-like storehouse outside space, time, and mentality. In this doctrine of two worlds, we draw on these perfect originals in this second world, an Urbs Beata, while encountering their faulty derivates in our comings and goings here on

---

[55] From "Wild Geese"

Earth. The "mother" swoons and the "father" admits his admiration
of the "floral pattern" of a Beacon Hill "sofa," too. They are recalling
"beauty" from up above to appreciate its fluctuating representation
as not only a couch but also the Grand Canyon, a tightrope walker,
purple tulip. How our own perfect forms flicker in Plato's funny heaven
when parents say of themselves as parents, We did the best we could,
and children unconsciously scan the furniture in advance of the messes
they're bound to make.

If Mary Oliver is a *permission poet*, is she a *peripatetic poet*, too, going
around on foot to gather her materials and vibes? Entering the woods of
Cuyahoga County as a child, and, as an adult, walking up on Blackwater
Pond near Cape Code's tip where a blacksnake holds its head above
water long enough to be born into one of her poems, is she another kind
of poet, too? She once said,

> I've written before that God has 'so many names.' To me, it's
> all right if you look at a tree, as the Hindus do, and say the
> tree has a spirit. It's a mystery, and mysteries don't compromise
> themselves—we're never gonna know. I think about the
> spiritual a great deal. I like to think of myself as a praise poet.
> I acknowledge my feeling and gratitude for life by praising the
> world and whoever made all these things.[56]

Of the fifteen collections of poems Mary Oliver wrote, the one before
Dream Work, titled *American Primitive*, won the Pulitzer. When it
appeared, she was already being touted as the bestselling poet in modern
times. Here I must resist the adolescent notion that Oliver's popularity
has anything to do with my impatience with her poetry. Am I envious?
I hate the idea of my being envious. When I read from her poem about
the geese—"Tell me about despair, yours, and I will tell you mine. /
Meanwhile the world goes on"—I envy not so much the lines themselves
as the *certainty* in the world she evokes. The speaker is so untroubled
that she may offer true catharsis to a reader. Her poems, nature poems
in our time of changing weather patterns, may recall the sound of water
insinuating a rivulet in a narrow valley in such ways that we may ask,

---

[56] From the 2011 interview with Maria Shriver

Can someone please explain what's the matter with a single, solitary world with no other world to mirror it?

Mary Oliver's poems are not all about nature. In *Dream Work*, she leaves the woods of her youth to write in about her own suffering. The poem "Rage" is about a man, presumably her father, sexually abusing with her when she is a child. Of him she writes,

> But you were also the red song
> in the night,
> stumbling through the house
> to the child's bed,
> to the damp rose of her body,
> leaving your bitter taste.

The damp rose and its pretty connotations warn me off this poem for obvious and, I think, inarticulable reasons. I may say that I cannot place "red song in the night" in relation to anything concrete about her father's actions or her suffering, when in fact I feel something of the taboo and compare it with a relatively innocuous experience in my own upbringing. As a boy, I drove my own father to withdraw into himself, and this was my shortcoming. I took the "What if'" and "why…but then why" of any child to manic extremes and talked him to death without realizing it. He hated what he called my What-if Questions so much as to demand my silence after I asked for how long and he said don't ask how long but starting now keep quiet.

Can someone please tell me what's the matter with a solitary, solo world with no other world to mirror it? Can someone please tell me what's the matter with a solitary, just world with no other world to mirror it? Can someone please tell me what's the matter with a lonely world with no other world to mirror it? "Something in me still starves," writes Mary Oliver. "In what is probably the most serious inquiry of my life, I have begun to look past reason, past the provable, in other directions. Now I think there is only one subject worth my attention and that is the precognition of the spiritual side of the world and, within this recognition, the condition of my own spiritual state."[57] Can someone

---

[57] From her essay "Winter Hours"

please tell me what's the matter with a solitary, just world with no other world to mirror it? Can someone please tell me what's the matter with a solitary, just world with no other world to mirror it? Can someone please tell me what's the matter with a solitary, just world with no other world to mirror it?

If Mary Oliver wanders into the woods near Maple Heights with her pencils and handsewn notebook, she also sets these materials aside to whittle or spot animals or divert streams with rocks peeled from the moist earth. Whether or not she assembles a thatched house for a wayward girl leaving her real home forever, she writes her first poems at fourteen, graduates from her Maple Heights high school at seventeen or eighteen and, extracurricular to her secondary school experience, attends the Interlochen Arts Camp in Michigan as a percussionist in the National High School Orchestra. After graduation, in what reads like a fieldtrip to Austerlitz, New York, she befriends Edna St. Vincent Millay's sister, Norma, and together they pore over the papers of the erudite and lyrical big sister, Edna of the Roaring Twenties. Oliver does go to college, to Ohio State University and to Vassar, without taking degrees, then lives for fifty years in Provincetown with her partner Molly Cook, a photographer and gallery owner. Too soon, it must have seemed, do the women enter retirement together in Florida, where Oliver outlives Cook, and then comes a protracted mourning period for Oliver, as she contracts lymphoma and at eighty-three dies on the island of Hobe Sound.

As a child, Phædo is bursting with beautiful What-if Questions when an invading army, its hungry principals, enslaves him. Having destroyed his family home in Elis as part of the Elean War, the Spartans murder his parents, leaving him eternally eighteen in the pages of *The Phaedo of Plato*. He has been sold to the owner of a house of male prostitution when the news arrives that Socrates is ransoming him. Does Socrates buy him for his looks alone? Does Phædo say something clever in their first meeting? The story of an orphan finding his way into a school so famous as to survive in our collective consciousness represents the chance of a lifetime. Of all possible forms, this one appeals to me most—*the chance of a lifetime*. Meanwhile, the versatile actor Phædo is capturing with his moves and his voice the men in Phlius converging on the site of Socrates's death. I imagine Mary Oliver going back and forth as to whether she should join them. Without her Ohioan future in place, she takes the place of Evenus, a famous poet in Athens, in my imagination. She is he before her childhood bed has slipped into existence in the Twentieth Century, before the soft animals of our contemporary bodies have for the first time stretched, before those wild geese can grant permission by their flight.

Mary Oliver isn't with Socrates when he dies, but she is nearby. Ever the impersonator, Phædo comes along afterwards to do his uncanny Socrates as a way of relaying to her their condemned teacher's final words: "Crito," he says. As was Socrates' manner, he looks fixedly at her as if she is their friend Crito and not Mary. "We owe a cock to Asclepius. Pay it and don't forget." Phædo gets the pitch right—womanly—and the lilts, quick vowels, proud silences. If his performance is premature, for Socrates drank hemlock only an hour before, it is his way of dealing with the pain of intolerable loss. Unable to take his savior's place or to embalm him like an Egyptian, he makes this awkward reanimation.

Phædo performs in silence Xanthippe's arrival at the prison with one of the sons after the order has come down to kill her husband. It isn't their eldest, Lamprocles, who has Socrates' looks, but a younger boy, Sophroniscus or Menexenus, who shares his mother's nose. Xanthippe is crying, and her boy, Phædo's acting makes clear, is confused when his father, breaking Phædo's silence, explains his enthusiasm for his own death:

> And now, O my judges, I desire to prove to you
> that the real philosopher has reason
> to be of good cheer when he is about to die,
> and that after death he may hope
> to obtain the greatest good in the other world.

An imaginary Mary Oliver wants to know why he must be so cold about it. Is he the repressed father who chooses death over new earthly beginnings? Why not stay for the sake of your loved ones? Why forsake your memories of your wife and children and your crew gathered daily at the Agora to die by the rhetoric of some unknowable process? Is his sense of belonging elsewhere not more like the renunciations one associates with depression? An imaginary Mary Oliver knows him. A depressed dad from a certain generation would deny he's depressed, or wouldn't realize it. Call this a lack of insight when he cannot sense what about him everyone's picking up on.

Integral to her contemplation of death as the separation of the mind from the body so the soul can lift away like a wild goose or hawk, the imaginary Mary Oliver is drawn by abstractions through the emotional climes she seeks in her comprehension of mortality. At her side, Phædo's Socrates explains that his death will be an erotic encounter, the confirmation he aches for—perfection. The noun is perfection to fill the nighttime sky with light. When he speaks of it, he sounds like a frenetic child overflowing with What-if Questions, so breathless she wants to ignore him. If the idiot had agreed to her plan to slip from his jailcell in the middle of the night onto any Athens street corner, and he'd gone on the run as she'd asked, would he still be a valid teacher? She used to imagine greeting him in the moonlight as he lifted a cover over his head and emerged from a manhole into the role of bandit. She supplies him with map, money, a little food, a secret address, a bicycle for a speedier getaway. When I was a child, I clipped a playing card in my spokes' orbit to make pedaling sound like a paper motor.

Long before the coming of the Paraclete, those fellows living more in their heads than their hearts or bodies took déjà vu, lucid dreaming, the mystery of their own creative output, and a nagging sense of elsewhere as evidence for a second world above. Writes the actual Mary Oliver: "The second world—the world of literature—offered me, besides the pleasures of form, the sustentation of empathy (the first step of what Keats called negative capability) and I ran for it. I relaxed in it. I stood willingly and gladly in the characters of everything—other people, trees, clouds. And this is what I learned: that the world's *otherness* is antidote to confusion, that standing *within* this otherness—the beauty and the mystery of the world, out in the fields or deep inside books—can re-dignify the worst-stung heart."[58] Before any savior-type arrives, heady men and women must take garden-variety mystical experiences as hard evidence for the existence of ethereal sanctuaries.

Please imagine Athens again as Phædo, in the role of Crito, offers the god of medicine a rooster to cure a dead teacher of what he calls the sickness of life. The imaginary Mary Oliver asks how a man with three loyal sons, a loyal wife, loyal friends, and the loyalest of loyal students can think of living as a chronic illness? She's nothing next to him, in

---

[58] From her essay "Staying Alive"

terms of reputation, yet she embraces life as a vast array of poignancies that like notes on a lyre include fading as part of their splendor. When she shares such optimism with the men, they smile and wink at each other, as if to signal that she will only ever be melancholic. She has to laugh. If he ever did one, Phædo's impersonation of her would reveal a lightness of spirit that the men's ingrained view of her can't allow for.

Seems only yesterday and some twenty-five centuries before the lifetime in which she writes *Dream Work*—a book about dogfish, wild trilliums, morning ritual, the Shoshone and Arapaho of the Wind River Reservation, milkweed, Beethoven, a shark, clams, wild geese— that an imaginary Mary Oliver, an urban poet among urban poets, learned the names of flowers as a way of stretching herself beyond her habitual subject matter of the deterioration of marriages and sophisticated love affairs flaring up in foundering metropolises. "See this aster here," she says to no one in particular. "These peonies, this Christmas rose." Flowers are good for taking her mind off the topic of mute and singing fathers. She will remain an urbanite a little longer, so let the heads of flowers, their blooms, their petals, remind her less of nature and more of brass horns, the trumpet-playing competitions popular on every Athens Commons.

What is the red song of a thirty-something patriarch whispering and here bellowing? Where may redness go as it recedes? My own pulse quickens recalling my long, questioning past. Of her memory of her father somehow going home from the ice-skating rink without her and doubling back once he realizes, Mary Oliver explains, "When [he] came through the door, I thought—never had I seen so handsome a man; he talked, he laughed, his movements were smooth and easy, his blue eyes were clear. He had simply, he said, forgotten that I existed.... I put on my coat, and we got into the car, and he sat back in the awful prison of himself, the old veils covered his eyes, and he did not say another word." Does the red song of a young father oscillate in volume and flicker on and off again? What is the redness of song to senses other than hearing?

Some see sadness planted on the forehead of the imaginary Mary Oliver. Phædo sees it but until recently has been too kind to say. The other men see it and don't hesitate to say. Socrates saw, without ever saying. If she really is unhappy, and she doubts she is, she blames it on the pressure

of finding her true calling. In ancient Athens and not in new Ohio
or Provincetown or Hobe Sound, she passes the time writing poems
no one cares to read. They spring more from her head than her heart,
and they do not *spring*, for she extracts them like mineral ore from a
mountainside. But the poems are not yet about mountains. Uppity city
folk argue, cheat, and hoard while Pelion and the herons at Lake Prespa
wait for her attention.

But behold Asphodelus. This grey plant dominates the fields of
the land of the dead and may be the food of the dead, too. When
Mary Oliver tells Socrates about this, instead of engaging her in a
conversation about mythical flowers, he explains his poison. The
hemlock tea he drinks to end his life comes from the shrub hemlock
and not those mythical conifers whose dense blue shade reminds Mary
Oliver inexplicably of milk. Rising from smooth, green stocks, the
shrubs that store the poison have triangular leaves clearly marked with
streaks of red and purple as warning signs of their toxicity. Pestle comes
to mind, and mortar, for what could be a more primal example of a
misshapen thing in our present world and its perfect original sitting
in a second-world gallery? Ground-down leaves for a philosopher's tea
smell like parsnips. Once in your blood stream, the alkaloid coniine,
resembling nicotine in schematics, confounds your central nervous
system and you stop breathing.

Behaving like the historical Evenus, an imaginary Mary Oliver is so
upset with Socrates that she doesn't go to the prison to hear his final
talk on immortality. Imagine. Someone so central to your creative and
intellectual life, and you let your ego get in the way of saying goodbye.
Mary Oliver sends Cebes in her place. He's the one to lodge her
complaint, which Phædo enacts now: "Socrates," he says, "in the time
since you were sentenced to death, why this sudden interest in writing
poems? Why at the last-minute upstage our good friend Mary Oliver?
She is our hometown poet, not you. She's dedicated her life to it. You're
our philosopher. You're well established." While Mary Oliver waits for
Cebes to report back, Phædo's Socrates looks from his jail cell beyond
the men encircling him and says in a tone of derangement, "Behold the
herons down along the tideline." He freezes and she awaits Socrates'
apology. He says instead, "The Athenians are killing me today," and a
long-held silence washes over the crowd. The wind blows in the trees.

Phædo cannot stay in character lamenting Socrates' unwillingness to acknowledge that he will not see them anymore. Playing the role of Socrates again, he makes eye contact with one imaginary man after another. "Say goodbye to Mary Oliver for me," he says in her absence. "Tell her, if she is wise, to follow me as soon as possible."

A recurring dream informs Socrates that his true calling is to compose music. "I've always assumed my philosophical tracts satisfied this demand for music," Phædo recounts in his voice, "but after my conviction, I began to worry. Was I taking my pesky dream seriously enough?" Not only do we survive our deaths, he tells us, but we vaguely comprehend that all knowledge is recollection. Today's wunderkind starts blowing his horn a lifetime before coming into the body of the person who invents his own orchestra. Yesteryear's city poet may write to us many years from now about rising sea levels, the extinction of the dodo bird, migration refugees. Socrates must make music so as not to anger the gods while he wagers for the most musical new life possible. But he can't write music, can he? Despite his enormous ego, he admits as much. He will obey the dream by writing poems to be sung to the accompaniment of a lyre upon his departure.

Socrates hardly tolerates poets as his own Plato would bar them from the Perfect City. Still, he must shadow the imaginary Mary Oliver in her craft. If she dabbles in nature writing in their native Greece, he dabbles in nature. If she experiments with flowers, he experiments with flowers. Because good poets tell good stories, he'll steal a great one as his passport into his next situation. He borrows animal stories from Aesop and breaks them into lines and novel patterns of sound and meaning to lubricate himself to squeeze through a celestial opening into the Palace of Forms. But is he making the grade with the gods of our day? Does he write a single singable poem? Will she remember the name Euterpe in Cleveland? So begins their arrangement of strips of prose whose natural curls flatten out by the knives of their hands into Aesop's heron's that they may their own:

> [A hunter of her own breakfast,
> a heron walking beside a stream
> watches over food like a brood.]

[She is childless.]
[Her neck long,
eyes made cruel for stalking,
she cocks her head back
and her bill like a clapping javelin.]
[Streams aswarm with ignorant swimmers.]
[Crossing into their lines of sight,
she stands refracted there,
quavering, odd, tower-like,
when a small body passes through her shadow.]
["I wouldn't eat you," she says,
if you were the last perch on earth."]
[You're too puny a morsel."]
[Seeing no fish whatsoever in the blinding sun,
Great Fisher settles on a snail diet beside no great pond.]
[Do not to be too hard to please
if you don't want a mollusk for your rations.][59]

The quick-flying soul glimpses all the things those abstract nouns stand for, forgetting most but not all of what its keeper once beheld and in prior persons engendered. "For whatever reason," writes Mary Oliver, "the heart cannot separate the world's appearance and actions from morality and valor, and the power of every idea is intensified, if not actually created, by its expression in substance. Over and over in the butterfly we see the idea of transcendence. In the forest we see not the inert but the aspiring. In water that departs forever and forever returns, we experience eternity." [60] Like a swift the quick-flying soul tumbles through parcels of forever. A swift the quick-flying soul catches glimpses. Soul is swift but lingers. To catch it is to play with each other. Please do come up softly everywhere it rests. Go away as if you never left.

The blue herons returned to Magee Marsh on the south shore of Lake Erie a week earlier than anyone thought they would. They arrived at the

---

[59] A strange but true story, Socrates was appropriating Aesop's animal stories and arranging them into different forms in an attempt to become a poet some gods could admire in their consideration of his afterlife.

[60] From the essay "Wordsworth's Mountain," published in *Long Life: Essays and Other Writings*

Bath Road heronry, between Akron Peninsula and River roads, around
the middle of February. They usually nest in secluded spots. The way
we crowd the Earth, one wonders what we're getting them used to.
One wonders at the way we crowd the Earth. The way we crowd. Mary
Oliver writes early in the Twenty-first Century: "I sit at the edge of Great
Pond. The morning light strikes the mist and begins to dispel it. On the
pond two geese are floating. Beneath them their reflected images glide;
between them five goslings have only recently emerged from the grassy
hummock of birth and already they are slipping along eagerly on this
glassy road."[61] In "One or Two Things," Mary Oliver writes,

> For years and years, I struggled
> just to love my life. And then
>
> The butterfly
> rose, weightless, in the wind.
> "Don't love your life
> too much," it said,
>
> and vanished
> into the world.[62]

A butterfly drags its refutation of our shortcomings across shapely life.
Some scouts are deranged until they can make sense of their earthly
surroundings. Phædo's mashups of men's voices into what sounds like
a chatty circle of friends cannot convey that Socrates is short and snub-
nosed or that a cock is a funny thing to owe. Small-mouthed Socrates
sticks a square of rolling paper on his lip and pulls it way, cupping it
with his fingers to roll with tobacco. He's asking around for a light when
his sons ask him for butterfly kisses at bedtime, the smell of smoke on
his breath part of his homecoming. Ohio is pastoral. It's nice. A pair
of butterflies flaps about the milkweed along a dry creek bed. More
like a constant feeling than endless acts of personification, a forest is
an extended family and, more important than most people, not a one-
time production featuring what Dad calls A-list players. The sky is the
least memorable and biggest thing one can encounter. Great Pond is

------

[61] From the essay "The Ponds"
[62] From the poem "One or Two Things," originally published *Dream Work*

what they long to see but cannot remember. "I, too, live in this ordinary world," writes Mary Oliver. "I was born into it. Indeed, most of my education was intended to make me feel comfortable within it. Why that enterprise failed is another story. Such failures happen, and then, like all things, are turned to the world's benefit, for the world has a need for dreamers."[63] Phædo's Socrates has not drunk yet. Or he can drink again to refine his performance. He raises his legs up to rub his ankles as imaginary jailers loosen his fetters. Thank you, thank you. He rubs his wrists and, looking up at the men, places his feet flat on the ground, pausing as if to regain his composure. Will Phædo act out each crying man before he's finished or will it be one composite crier? Working himself into character he says, "When I arrived at the jail this morning, I felt detached from myself. Mine was a detached grief, Mary, when suddenly it hit me that our teacher was about to die. I became acutely aware of my surroundings." Mary Oliver writes a bird poem that begins,

> This morning
> > the hawk
> > > rose up
> > > > out of the meadow's browse
>
> and swung over the lake[64]

She writes a second one about a heron and holds in her mind a third about the downy owl on moonless nights. If on such a night I write something out of a sense of pain I am at a loss to identify, I am equally dismayed by the reality of Mary Oliver's own pain and my inability to register it through her poems. If I'd known I would grow critical of her work or envy her conviction in the existence of such pure ideals as love, mirth, praise, and constancy, I might not have picked her poems in the first place. If I would have cried as a boy, I seem only to blush now. When I try to teach myself appreciation for a Mary Oliver poem, a faraway beauty, one rarely close to me, takes the form of a hawk rising from the tender shoots upon which animals graze when their executioner is not waiting. Something is missing though. The hawk is closer to the

---

[63] From her essay "Of Power and Time"
[64] Mary Oliver includes the poem "Hawk" in *New and Selected Poems: Volume One* (1992).

moon than to me as it flies. Closer to the sun and to every celestial body. Because I don't seem to have life-altering moments of perception, even with such bodies in mind, I must go last on a list of those who will become enlightened. I do want the enlightenment that "Wild Geese" offers, and I don't. I'm always in my head contradicting myself like this until things start to feel real again. Socrates is dead. Mary Oliver is dead. Reading myself all but out of existence, I feel myself being slowly replaced by the imperceptible movements of animals across a darkening plain, beneath a long horizontal line of light fading with the horizon.

Say Nothing

Up the hill stands an observatory three and a half turns from lock to lock. Field flowers fill the slope. Roots grow far from the bunker. I believe it all except for the lopsidedness of the halves, learned speech and handmade dances, the particulars drawn freehand.

Taking up lying down rails, casting a new track, section hands on the line down from Sac follow the wagon tracks into Chinatown. Ophir City. Take my eyes long enough to go back down and collect the scatter. Hear the news of our sorrowful brother. Hear of his death while I eat. Morning gathers our family, sisters, brothers, mothers, fathers, before a place setting, a preacher. Walk after them, keep them in sight, an open book in rising light.

I was entering the lyrical when I thought, confession, sensate, senate. The soft paper comes apart in milk. The countryside is weeping two parts light one part dark. Squall, sun-shower, next season's escalade. I was entering the lyrical when I thought

to hold something rare, polestar, wind-harp, a gathering for stew, a box of archives floating in space. I wonder now if my body is coming with me. But get me deeper into the afternoon. Rise up to a single body. The beautiful forms of empty, the clouds and all who befriended those who knew

the star I have come to see, the first star of night, light ready to blaze, bereft, the glorious god with the stumbling one. Walking beside a line of trees, wooden men, men of straw. Exploring breaking in various forms. Oaks and barns turn in the wood.

Up the hill stands an observatory. Do you recall our first time here? We entered softly, let evenings go by and by. The things you said tonight I'll remember forever. My only request had been that you say nothing. But sweep on again, singing through the big places.

Sources—for further reading

"Preface"

- Hejinian, Lyn, and Barrett Watten. *A Guide to Poetics Journal: Writing in the Expanded Field, 1982-1998*, Wesleyan University Press, 2013.
- Keats, John, and Hyder Edward Rollins. *The Letters of John Keats. Volume 1: 1814-1818*, Cambridge University Press, 2012.
- Panagiotidou, Maria-Eirini. *The Poetics of Ekphrasis*, Springer Nature, 2022.
- Perloff, Nancy. *Concrete Poetry: A 21st-Century Anthology*, Reaktion Books, 2022.

"Euphemisms for Seasonal Affective Disorder"

- Johnson, Robert Flynn. *Days in a Life: The Art of Tetsuya Noda*, San Francisco: Asian Art Museum, 2004.

"#HarmoniousRelationsThusLaidBare"

- Kozhamthadam, Job. *The Discovery of Kepler's Laws: The Interaction of Science, Philosophy, and Religion*, University of Notre Dame Press, 1994.

"March Sentences in Response to Apples"

- George-Warren, Holly. *Janis: Her Life and Music*, Simon & Schuster, 2019.
- McClure, Michael. *Ghost Tantras*. City Lights Publishers, 2013.

"Upon Leaving the Botanical Gardens (Golden Gate Park, San Francisco)"

- Evans, Margiad. *A Ray of Darkness*, Calder Publishing, 1952.
- Head, Bessie. *Tales of Tenderness and Power*, Heinemann International Incorporated, 1990.
- Sarton, May. *Journal of a Solitude*, W. W. Norton & Company, 1992.
- Shakespeare, William, et al. *The Folger Library General Reader's Shakespeare*, Washington Square Press, 1957.

"Jaunt"

- Armantrout, Rae. *Veil: New and Selected Poems*, Wesleyan University Press, 2001.
- Messerli, Douglas. *"Language" Poetries: An Anthology*. New Directions Publishing Corporation, 1987.

"Mood for a Day"

- Hamilton, Ann. *corpus (with an essay by Lawrence Raab)*, MASS MoCA, 2004.
- Langer, Susanne. *Mind: An Essay on Human Feeling*, The Johns Hopkins University Press, 1988.
- Wallach, Amei. "A Conversation with Ann Hamilton in Ohio," *American Art*, 2008.

"A Dun Forest"

- Blake, William, & Smith, Patti. *William Blake: Poems (Selected by Patti Smith)*, Vintage Books, 2006.

"Ringtones"

▶ Blofeld, John. *Bodhisattva of Compassion: The Mystical Tradition of Kuan Yin*, Shambhala, 2009.
▶ Niditch, Susan. *Judges: a commentary,* Westminster John Knox Press, 2008.
▶ Steinbeck, John, *The Pastures of Heaven*, Penguin Classics, 1995.

"Some Boys"

▶ Driscoll, Christopher M, et al. *Kendrick Lamar and the Making of Black Meaning*, Routledge, 2020.
▶ Spellman, Ched. *Irenaeus: Essential Readings*, Fontes Press, 2023.

"Will You Name Yourselves"

▶ Berthoff, Ann E. *The Making of Meaning: Metaphors, Models, and Maxims for Writing Teachers*, Boynton/Cook Publishers, 1981.
▶ Ginsberg, Allen, and Bill Morgan. *Deliberate Prose: Selected Essays, 1952-1995*, Perennial, 2001.
▶ Golubski, Christina. "Beneath the Tamarind Tree: Nigeria and the Resilience of the Chibok Girls," *Brookings*, 2019.
▶ Whitman, Walt, et al. *Song of Myself: With a Complete Commentary.* Iowa City University Of Iowa Press, 2016.

"Some Flags"

▶ Day, Dorothy, et al. *The Long Loneliness: The Autobiography of the Legendary Catholic Social Activist*, Harperone, 1952.
▶ Gilchrist, Anne, and Walt Whitman. *The Letters of Anne Gilchrist and Walt Whitman*, Good Press, 2019.
▶ Ginsberg, Allen. "I saw the three fish one head," *The Catholic Worker*, 1967.

"In Memory of Alice Neel (1900-1984)"

- Neel, Alice, et al. *Alice Neel: People Come First.* New York, The Metropolitan Museum Of Art, 2021.
- Neel, Alice, et al. *At Home: Alice Need in the Queer World*, David Zwirner Books, 2024.

"Greta in the Popular Imagination"

- Hourdequin, Marion Elizabeth. "Intergenerational ethics, moral ambivalence, and climate change," *The Harvard Review of Philosophy*, 2022.
- Thunberg, Greta, et al. *Our House Is on Fire: Scenes of a Family and a Planet in Crisis*, Penguin Books, 2020.

"I Am Against Driving Myself Crazy"

- Lax, Robert, and Thomas Kellein. *33 Poems*. New York, New Directions Publishing Corporation, 2019.
- Finlay, Ian Hamilton, and Alec Finlay. *Ian Hamilton Finlay: Selections*, University Of California Press, 2012.
- Merton, Thomas. *New Seeds of Contemplation*. New York, New Directions Book, 2007.

"At the Height of the Pandemic (Days of 2020)"

- Finley, James. *The Contemplative Heart*, Sorin Books, 2000.
- Konstantinos Petrou Kabaphes, and Constantine Cavafy. *The Complete Poems of Cavafy*, Houghton Mifflin Harcourt, 1976.

"The Lute of Memory"

► Ashbery, John. *Three Books: Poems*, Penguin Books, 1993.

► O'Hara, Frank, and Donald Allen. *The Collected Poems of Frank O'Hara*, University Of California Press, 1995.

► Peacock, Thomas Love, et al. *Peacock's Four Ages of Poetry; Shelley's Defence of Poetry; Browning's Essay on Shelley.* Norwood Editions, 1978.

► Walser, Robert. *A Schoolboy's Diary and Other Stories.* New York Review of Books, 2013.

"West, Evening (Regulus)"

► Engelman, Siegfried and Elaine Bruner. "The Pet Goat," *Reading Mastery II: Rainbow Edition*, Macmillan/McGraw-Hill, 1995.

► García, Mario T. *A Dolores Huerta Reader*, University of New Mexico Press, 2008.

► Hansberry, Lorraine. *A Raisin in the Sun*, Spark Publishing, 1959.

► Huang, Marijane. *Beyond Two Worlds*, AuthorHouse, 2017.

► Maarek, Gérard. *An Introduction to Karl Marx's Das Kapital: A Study in Formalisation*, Oxford University Press, 1979.

► Piketty, Thomas. *Capital in the Twenty-First Century*, Harvard University Press, 2014.

► Viramontes, Helena María. *Under the Feet of Jesus*, Penguin, 1996.

► Whitman, Walt. *Complete Poetry and Collected Prose*, Literary Classics Of The United States, 1982.

► Wolf, Margery. *Women and the Family in Rural Taiwan*, Stanford University Press, 1972.

► Yates, Frances A. *The Art of Memory*, The Bodley Head, 2014.

"Wonder Woman Alights on Dominican School"

- Gorey, Edward. *The Vinegar Work: Three Volumes of Moral Instruction; the Gashlycrumb Tinies; the Insect God; the West Wing*, Simon And Schuster, 1963.
- Lepore, Jill. *The Secret History of Wonder Woman*, Melbourne Scribe, 2015.

"Virgin Territory"

- Dos Passos, John. *The Big Money*, Houghton Mifflin Harcourt, 2013.
- Steinbeck, John. *Travels with Charley: In Search of America*, Penguin Books, 2017.

"Before the Advent"

- Christensen, Paul. *Minding the Underworld: Clayton Eshleman & Late Postmodernism*, Black Sparrow Press, 1991.
- Eshleman, Clayton. *Fracture*, Black Sparrow Press, 1983.

"New Barber"

- Capote, Truman. *The Grass Harp: Including a Tree of Night and Other Stories*, Vintage International/Vintage Books, 2012.
- Stein, Gertrude, and Joan Retallack. *Gertrude Stein: Selections*, University of California Press, 2008.

"The Mountain Protagonist"

- Adler, Alfred. *What Life Could Mean to You*. Richmond, Oneworld, 2009.
- Kishimi, Ichiro, and Koga Fumitake. *The Courage to Be Disliked: How to Free Yourself, Change Your Life and Achieve Real Happiness*, Allen & Unwin, 2019.

"Reading Plato in Memory of Mary Oliver (1935-2019)"

- Aesopus, et al. *Aesop's Fables: Complete and Unabridged*, Wordsworth Classics, 1995.
- Hass, Robert. *Human Wishes*. Ecco Press, 2011.
- Oliver, Mary. *Blue Pastures*. Houghton Mifflin Harcourt, 1995.
    - ---. *Dream Work*. Penguin, 2024.
    - ---. *New and Selected Poems*: *Volume 1*, Beacon Press, 1992.
    - ---. *Winter Hours: Prose, Prose Poems, and Poems*, Houghton Mifflin Company, 2000.
- Plato, and Benjamin Jowett. *The Dialogues of Plato*. Oxford, Clarendon Press, 1969.
- Shriver, Maria. "Maria Shriver Interviews the Famously Private Poet Mary Oliver." *Oprah.com*, 2011.

Acknowledgements

I begin with Ingrid, who sits beside me now. Thank you. I am also grateful to my parents Marcia and John, and my siblings Michael and Laura, for encouraging me in my creative endeavors. I also write in memory of my late aunt; Fran Booth, who passed away unexpectedly in 2022, was always excited about my writing. She would have liked seeing this book. Her daughter Jennifer is here, and for this I am grateful.

I wish to thank poet and publisher Michael Poage and his colleagues at Blue Cedar Press for their embrace of hybrid writing. I cannot adequately express my gratitude to the poet and fiction writer Linda Michel-Cassidy for her copyediting prowess. Writer and artist Catherine Brady played an essential role in shaping this book. My colleague by way of the Bay Area's Writing Salon and the Marin Poetry Center, poet and educator Erin Rodoni also gave me extensive feedback on some of the more fraught drafts of what finally emerged. Much thanks, too, to poet Amanda Moore for her collegiality and her invitation to the Cahoots Residency.

Two luminaries of my life: novelist and poet Elizabeth Costello, whose facilitation of Ekphrastival in Portland, Oregon, exposes more and more people to writing about art, and to Monica Regan, whose work as a poet, artist, and advocate for immigrants' rights keeps me in mind of creative responses to injustice. I also feel lucky to know the writers in my old writing group, the Drunken Goats. In particular, Stephanie Vernier, Frank Dowling, and Karma Bennett followed my first forays into what were then my new approaches to poetical writing. I acknowledge here, too, my early writing teacher Lissa McLaughlin in Madison.

Finally, I want to name some folks whose influence I cherish: Steven Kahn, Karl Soehnlein, Larry Ebert, Cesar Love, Jennifer Kramer, Vince Feher, Laird Harrison, Karen Laws, Stephanie Vernier, Dennis Estrada, Andrew Dugas, Sarah Mullin, Bill Doak, Brad Champagne, Lewis Buzbee, Paul Pryor Lorentz, Brady Metcalfe, Mark Routhier, Lisa Perez, J.D. Kay, John Brennan, and Joey Carney.

David Booth
San Francisco, Calif.
March 2025